DANTE'S PARADISO

By DANTE ALIGHIERI

Translated by
HENRY WADSWORTH LONGFELLOW

Introduction by ELLEN M. MITCHELL

Dante's Paradiso (The Divine Comedy, Volume II, Paradise)
By Dante Alighieri
Translated by Henry Wadsworth Longfellow
Introduction by Ellen M. Mitchell

Print ISBN 13: 978-1-4209-7461-4
eBook ISBN 13: 978-1-4209-7628-1

Cover Image: a detail from a fresco at the Villa Massimo in Rome by Philipp Veit showing Dante and Beatrice speaking to the teachers of wisdom Thomas Aquinas, Albertus Magnus, Peter Lombard and Sigier of Brabant in the Sphere of the Sun, c. 1817-1827.

Please visit *www.digireads.com*

CONTENTS

Introduction

Hamilton Mabie says that "it is possible to spend years of study on what may be called the externals of the *Divina Commedia*, and remain unaffected in nature by this contact with one of the masterpieces of the spirit of man. It is also possible to so absorb Dante's thought and so saturate one's self with the life of the poem as to add to one's individual capital of thought and experience all that the poet discerned in that deep heart of his and wrought out of that intense and tragic experience."

"Still studying Dante?" was the question of a visitor of Lowell. "Yes, always studying Dante," was the reply of one of the greatest scholars America has produced.

Four chief subjects occupy the inner life of Dante, the circle of his thoughts and feelings; politics, philosophy, love, faith. All are found harmoniously united in his great poem. The world of ideas in which he lived, the contents of the real world which surrounded him, are poured into one form and molded into one thought, the *Divina Commedia*. The writer's own life is chronicled in it, the transient names and local factions and forgotten crimes of his own day, as well as the mysteries of time and eternity. Dante comes near to us as an erring human soul, tempted, purified, and at last triumphant. Under the figure of his own experience, the unity of the visible and the invisible is vividly shadowed forth. This is the subject of the *Divina Commedia*,—the harmony between the divine and the human, between faith and reason, between God and the world.

Taken literally, Dante's poem is an account of his journey through Hell, Purgatory, Paradise; interpreted spiritually, it is a revelation of what man is and of what his life means. The soul that sins is in Hell, seeking to cut itself off from the divine organism of which it is a part. The result is impotence and misery.

Sin produces torment by creating a corresponding environment of hatred and antagonism. To sin is to suffer, because sin is contrary to the true nature of the soul. The guilty man creates his own penalty; penalty is born of freedom. Hell is free-will arrayed against the divine order, and therefore cursed; Heaven is free-will working in harmony with the divine order, and therefore blessed. To make self the centre of the universe is Hell; to strive to subordinate self and do God's will through failure and repeated effort is Purgatory; to attain the end finally through divine help is Paradise. Freedom is grounded in our relation to God; it is to know and love and do His will.

The rushes on the shores of Purgatory that instantly spring up again when plucked symbolize the spiritual law; to give is to receive. They symbolize also that true humility which finds in pain a blessing so far as pain results from wrongdoing. Whoever recognized more clearly than Dante that it is something within us rather than something outside of us that causes our unrest and dissatisfaction? To forgive our own faults is as necessary to spiritual growth as to forgive the faults of others. It is false humility to despise and depreciate one's self over much. "Blessed are the poor in spirit." But the poor in spirit are exalted inasmuch as they recognize their divine birthright, the dignity and worth of the human soul.

Purgatory is the school of aspiration and spiritual growth; what we aspire to be we are in some measure. We create in part our own environment; opportunity and temptation have only the power given them by the heart's desire. The higher law of heredity masters the lower; we are worms, as Dante says, but worms destined to form angelic butterflies.

By symbolism and music and picture, by direct and indirect teaching, we are constantly shown by Dante how we ascend by one another, and are at our best only when we take God's gifts for the benefit of those who, needing them, stand beyond us. Pain and inconvenience are angels in disguise to help us toward the joy of unselfish service. When God has blessed someone else through us then is his blessing truly ours. Greatness in man is this quality of taking into one's self and diffusing to others some part of the goodness and beauty and truth at the heart of the universe.

Pride, envy, anger, *accidia* or lukewarmness, gluttony and intemperance, lust,—the fatal roots in character of fatal deeds,—can only be exterminated by long continued effort and pain, rebelled against if one is in Hell, patiently and hopefully borne if one is in Purgatory. Pride as exclusiveness contradicts the very nature of spiritual good which cannot be monopolized by any soul. We grow by giving, not by keeping; to share is to increase our spiritual possessions.

Envy abuses the gift of spiritual sight and sees with grief the good of others. Men are envious because their desires are directed toward those things which exclude rather than include companionship. The few who possess material goods exclude from their possession the many; but the more there are who possess spiritual goods the more each one has and enjoys, "since good the more communicated the more abundant grows."

Anger obscures the duties we owe to others; lukewarmness makes us indifferent to evil; avarice and waste abuse our material means for helping men; gluttony and intemperance unfit us for human companionship; lust destroys the family, the element of social union. Sin is social as well as individual; its direct effect is to separate the sinner from the social whole in which he lives, and which by his deeds he would destroy. The true state of human beings is one of mutual love and service, giving and receiving the material products of the world, food, clothing, shelter; giving and receiving also feelings, thoughts, the experience of the race. Human life is vicarious, as Dr. William T. Harris has said, each one living through others and for others in a constant interchange of benefits. This is the truth seen by the regenerated self in Dante's Purgatory; this is the ideal realized in Dante's Paradise.

The gifts to men are various and by no means equal as regards material advantages and intellectual endowment. So, too, with environment; for one it is favorable to the growth of moral excellence, for another it is an atmosphere tending to vice and corruption. But whatever the gifts, whatever the environment, the human soul subsists apart as an independent being, not their creation but the creation of God, and therefore able to react upon limitations and convert them into freedom, transmuting evil into good. What we like is what we are; what we will is what we are struggling to become. To attain Paradise requires love as well as insight, fire as well as light. We may know and will rightly, but we must also feel rightly; we need an accession of the Christ-like spirit. Thirst for the divine has power to bear us upward; aspiration is the prophecy of attainment. What we crave and steadily seek will be ours, says Dante.

The *Paradiso* is the most difficult part of the *Divina Commedia*, but to one who comprehends its music, the music of spiritual life, the most inspiring. We are what we can see and realize. Dante, exiled, disappointed, embittered, sang those deathless songs of joy, so high and pure that the ear scarcely sustains their melody. He must have had in his heart the fountain of that joy, or he could not have interpreted so truly the fervor and love and high thought that are daily moving men and women to lead the spiritual life in obedience to Love Divine that rules hearts and sways the heavens in perpetual harmony.

"The glory of Him who moves all things penetrates through the universe, and shines in one part more and in another less," are Dante's opening words in the *Paradiso*. As the rays of the sun are received differently by different bodies, so with the goodness of God, which gives itself more and more as the capacity to receive it increases. The black clod absorbs and is warmed by the sunlight, but does not reflect and ray it forth on every side like the diamond, The gifts of God multiply by giving, and decrease by hoarding; he who gives most receives most. We are at our best only when we cheer and strengthen others with the help that has come to us; again and again Dante reiterates this truth.

Dante gives the exact time when he ascended to Paradise, April 13, 1300. He also describes its location according to the astronomical notions of his day. Is Heaven then a place according to Dante? What does he say? "Light and love enclose it;" "these near nor far nor add nor take away;" "it has no other where than the Divine mind." We must always look through the symbolism to interpret the poem aright.

Dante's ascent to Paradise after climbing the terraces of Purgatory is like the descent of a stream from a high mountain to its base. Rivers flow to the sea, but the soul of man rises to the stars, overcoming the downward gravitation of earth by the upward gravitation of spiritual desire and aspiration, the divine power of love.

Dante looks at Beatrice, Beatrice at the Sun, and the two are borne upward to the heaven of the Moon. "Within itself the eternal pearl received us, even as water receives a ray of light, remaining unbroken." A lower law is again replaced by a higher, the law of exclusion by that of inclusion, as the downward gravitation of matter by the upward gravitation of spirit. There is an exclusive sense in which I own houses and lands and material belongings, shutting out others from their possession; but knowledge and spiritual gifts increase as they are diffused and shared.

All the spirits in Dante's Paradise abide in the highest heaven, the Empyrean, but they show themselves to Dante in nine lower heavens that he may comprehend their different degrees of insight and beatitude. Gentle Piccarda Donati, in the heaven of the Moon, unfolds the secret of blessedness. It is not to desire a higher place, or to be thirsty for aught else than one has, since it is essential to heavenly existence to hold one's self within the divine will, " E la sua volontate è nostra pace." "And His will is our peace," says Piccarda, the finest single line in Dante's whole poem. Each soul has all the good it can hold and is unconscious of any lack; there is no jarring note in the heavenly harmony. Underlying diversity is perfect unity, the all-embracing bond of love, which moves each will in unison with the will of "Him who moves the Sun and the other stars."

On earth men are full of discontent because others excel them in material and intellectual gifts, envying their possessions and their happiness, discordant rather than harmonious notes in that social brotherhood which, like the brotherhood of saints, should rest on love, each rejoicing and participating in the good of all. The ideal shines before men,—true humility and content with what we have and are,—but it is an ideal slowly realized.

Piccarda's words to Dante burn with Love's heart of fire; listening to them, it is clear how "everywhere in Heaven is Paradise." Tending to the sea of divine love, insight and blessedness increase with sympathy and fellowship.

The Moon was known to Dante to shine with reflected light and to be nearest the earth. It is therefore symbolic of the souls who through defective will were compelled to break their religious vows, unable to defy circumstances and triumph over fear. We are what we are through inward defect rather than through outward environment.

In Mercury, veiled by the rays of the Sun, Dante meets the souls who have done great deeds for the sake of honor and fame, their motives of action tinged by selfishness, its reflection in the minds of others rather than in their own.

Lacking complete moral independence and freedom they rejoice in the principle of justice. The application of justice is the work of the law, hence the typical spirit in Mercury is Justinian. "Diverse voices make sweet notes," he says; "thus different degrees of joy contribute to harmony in Heaven," a thought often repeated by Dante. Let the star be content to shine as a star rather than to imitate the Sun. Is our place in life secondary, subordinate? If we do our work faithfully it is as genuine a contribution to the universal good as the work of greater men and women. We all contribute in different ways to a perfected society on earth and in heaven.

The earth's shadow ends on the surface of Venus, according to Ptolemy, Dante's astronomical authority. The souls in the Moon, in Mercury, in Venus, are overshadowed by earthly influences, shown in want of courage, worldly ambition, unregulated love; they are therefore excluded from the higher degree of blessedness. Loving, one learns the nature of love; seeking the good of others, one enters into the divine activity. But love must be for all men; it must strive to lift up into insight and blessedness the lowest dregs of humanity.

In Dante's fourth heaven of the Sun, the souls of the blessed are wholly self-illuminated. They form two great concentric circles, or wheels, revolving with different yet concordant motion, symbolizing unselfish individuality developed into a harmonious social whole. They are the great theologians and doctors of the church, who sought to prove that the Christian religion is identical with the results of sound knowledge and right thinking. Love radiates the resplendence with which they are clothed. Love comes from the vision of God, the light increasing with the ardor, the ardor with the vision. The more clearly one sees the divine, the more ardent the love; the more ardent the love, the clearer the vision. "Therefore the vision must perforce increase, increase the ardor which from that is kindled, increase the radiance which from this proceeds." To know God is to love Him; to love God is to know Him more completely.

> "O soaring soul! faint not nor tire!
> Each Heaven attained reveals a higher!"

In the fifth heaven of Mars, Dante sees the spirits, brightly scintillating, in the form of a cross, the supreme symbol of self-renunciation.

Up and down they move freely, but are never dissevered from the radiant fillet which binds them to the cross. As the spirits in the Sun show how knowledge increases love and love enkindles knowledge, the spirits in Mars renounce self utterly, their beneficent activity unobscured, by love of fame, as in Mercury. Bound to the cross and shining with its indwelling light, they are one with the whole of humanity.

Mars is the heaven of martyrs who have dared to be true to themselves; it is the heaven where Dante meets his great ancestor, Cacciaguida. Banishment from Florence, dependence, loneliness,—all these are foretold to the poet.

Journeying with Dante we have learned to know his soul, his pride and anger and bitterness, his desire for worldly power and fame,— faults that he humbly acknowledged and humbly sought to expiate. The voice of his heroic ancestors in Mars bids him conquer the cowardice that would lead him to suppress unwelcome truth, bids him "manifest his vision utterly." "Arise and conquer!" is the stirring cry from the spirits upgathered on the cross. Crucify selfish fear as well as pride and anger and ambition.

From the heaven of Mars, Dante and Beatrice rise to the heaven of Jupiter, the planet of righteous rulers who, arranged in the form of an eagle, comprise in luminous words the sentence: "*Diligete justitiam qui judicatis terram*" "Love justice, ye that be judges of the earth."

The eagle symbolizes the Holy Roman Empire—Dante's dream of a united nation based on, justice and law. When the eagle speaks, it "utters with its beak both I and My, when in conception it is We and Our," the idea seeming to be that the realization of the highest self is found in total humanity. Man as an individual is protected, guided, strengthened, and helped by others in the family, the State, the Church. The least can share in the triumphs of the greatest. In the large way we prosper or suffer together. Mars is fiery red, Jupiter silvery white; the ardor of love concentrated in sacrifice is found in one, the radiance of love beneficently diffused in the other.

One of the brightest lights in Jupiter is the Trojan Ripheus who, "through grace which distils from a fount so deep that creature never pushed the eye far as its primal wave, there below set all his love on righteousness, wherefore Faith, Hope and Charity were to him for baptism more than a thousand years before baptizing." Salvation is by faith, but faith is purely spiritual. "*Regnum coelorum* (the kingdom of heaven) suffereth violence from fervent love, and from that living hope that overcometh the Divine volition, not in the guise that man o'ercometh man, but conquers it because it will be conquered, and conquered, conquers by benignity."

Ascending from Jupiter to Saturn, Dante beholds a golden stairway, uplifted beyond the power of mortal vision, symbol of the life of mystical contemplation. Spheres of light, "becoming more beautiful with mutual rays," the souls in Saturn, enriched by the total experience of humanity, expand to the measure of the divine fullness.

Dante almost anticipates the jubilant cry of Beatrice as, entering the heaven of the Fixed Stars, she bids him

"Behold the hosts of Christ's triumphal march, and all the fruit
Harvested by the rolling of the spheres."

"Above myriads of lights, a sun was enkindling each and all of them, and through its living splendor the lucent substance shone so bright that I sustained it not," says Dante.

We pass from vision to doctrine, from the symbol to its essential meaning. What is Faith? What is Hope? What is Charity? The three must be ours in order to triumph over the world in a Christ-like spirit. To bear witness to the truth, to seek and save the lost, to overcome evil with good, to deal gently with the erring and sternly with the false, to suffer wrong rather than do wrong, to draw toward ourselves all forms of blessing in order to enrich the lives of others,—this is the triumph of the Christ-like spirit in man.

Rapt in the beauty of Beatrice, Dante rises to the swiftest and first-moved heaven, the *Primum Mobile*, where time and space both end. The increasing radiance in the eyes of Beatrice is like a mirror in which Dante beholds the reflection of new glory. She "*imparadises*" his mind. The more man is deepened in the contemplation of divine things, the higher he rises on the ladder of contemplation to God.

Dante sees a point infinitely small and infinitely bright, the symbolic manifestation of the divine nature, and round it nine concentric circles of fire, the nine angelic orders of the hierarchy of heaven. They are all upward gazing, and downward prevail, so that toward God they are all attracted and all attract,—a perfect symbol of the social ideal of Christ.

The ninth heaven is the heaven of influence, descending through Cherubim and Seraphim to the least and lowest who aspire toward a higher life. This is one of the deepest of Dante's lessons. We are to diffuse what we receive, to work forever to create the image of God in others as in ourselves. Love grows by giving; knowledge shared is knowledge deepened.

The primal light that irradiates all is received in as many modes; no two angels are precisely alike in their vision of God. "Wherefore since affection follows upon the act that conceives, the sweetness of love diversely glows and warms. Behold now the breadth and the height of the Eternal Goodness since it has made for itself so many mirrors on which it is broken, One in itself remaining as before."

In the ascent to the Empyrean Dante is over-powered by the greatness of his theme. He gives up the attempt to describe the beauty of Beatrice, "transcending measure." The Empyrean is the "Heaven which is pure light; light intellectual, full of love; love of true good, full of joy; joy which transcends every sweetness." Dante's first sensation is that of a flash of lightning, swathing him in a veil of its own effulgence. This is the welcome that "fits the candle to the flame," giving Dante the strength required for new insight. Men must be bathed in God's illuminating grace before their thirst for truth can be satisfied.

Raised to a higher power of vision, Dante sees "light in the form of a river, bright with effulgence, between two banks painted with a marvelous spring. Out of this stream were issuing living sparks, and on every side were setting themselves in the flowers, like rubies which gold encompasses. Then, as if inebriated by the odors, they plunged again into the wonderful flood, and as one was entering another was issuing forth." The river represents the grace and love of God; the ruby sparks are the angels; the flowers on the banks are the souls of the righteous; the movements represent the ministries of angels, ministries of joy and fellowship. All are images foreshadowing the truth.

As Dante bathes his eyes in the illuminating stream, its form changes, it flows in a circle consisting of a host of angelic beings, who form a great white rose. The petals of the rose are ranks of glorified saints, tier above tier, mirrored in the crystal sea of light, as a flower-clad hill is mirrored in a lake. The angels pass in a continual stream of glory between God and the saints, a glory consisting of knowledge and love, deepening to all eternity.

The imagery may have been suggested by the rose windows of Gothic cathedrals, or it may have spontaneously sprung up before Dante's creative imagination. "My vision lost not itself in the breadth and in the height, but took in all the quantity and the quality of that joy. There near and far nor add nor take away; for where God immediately governs, the natural law is of no relevancy."

Turning to speak to Beatrice, Dante finds an old man with pious mien, such as befits a tender father. It is St. Bernard, to whom it was given to be master of the hearts of men as St. Thomas Aquinas was of their intellects. Beatrice has returned to her place as a petal of the White Rose of Paradise. Raising his eyes upward, Dante beholds her "as she makes for herself a crown, reflecting from herself the eternal rays." What a sublime image! The glory of God penetrates the universe, blessing in proportion as it is accepted and reflected.

Beatrice, transcending all her words with the sweet splendor of her smile, is dear to us as the type of divine wisdom. She is dear to us also as the spirit of a love immortally famous, a love that once drew human breath like ours, and was pierced with the pain of sorrow and bereavement. Dante rises from circle to circle in the "*Paradiso*" by gazing on her loving eyes, always turned upward, drawing her lover from herself to God. The glance of Beatrice once fell on Dante's heart in Florence like a benediction. She died, and the poet's lady on earth became his lady in heaven. The love of his youth was to him a "New

Life," "*Vita Nuova*," an ideal followed through failure and error until in repentant devotion he is at last saved "as by fire." For what is the ideal but a guide, like the love of Beatrice, leading us closer and closer to the real, the beatific vision of God?

Dante's sight enters more and more into the rays of the high light which in itself is true. Memory and speech alike fail to reproduce the vision. He remembers an ineffable intuition, an ineffable sweetness to bear witness to his experience. "O abundant Grace, whereby I presumed to fix my eyes through the Eternal Light so far that there I consumed my sight." "Bound with love in one volume," Dante sees the essential and the accidental, the universal and the particular, whatever on earth is manifold and separated existing in God as parts of an organic whole.

Wholly rapt, gazing fixed, motionless and intent, Dante grows more and more enkindled. Within the deep and luminous subsistence of the lofty light, three circles appear of threefold color and of one dimension, the first reflected by the second, and the third as fire which from the one and from the other is equally breathed forth. The second circle, regarded closer, depicts within itself the human effigy. First, the mystery of the Trinity is revealed, one nature and essence in three persons; then the mystery of the human incarnated in the divine. Dante sees a human form and features, "perfect God and perfect man," in the "Light of Light."

The end crowns the work. Dante wishes to see how the image accords with the circle, the human nature with the divine, but recognizes that the wings of his intellect are unequal to the task. Then, suddenly smitten by a flash of illuminating grace, the truth is revealed. "To my high fantasy here power failed; but now my desire and my will, like a wheel which evenly is moved, the Love was turning which moves the Sun and the other stars."

Love, then, is Dante's solving word, love which shows us the way to the stars, the heights of Heaven. This is the end of man,—to climb through every phase of human experience to that region where the true, the good, and the beautiful blend in the white light of God. Beyond the horizon of speculation floats, in the passionless splendor of the Empyrean, a citadel of refuge for souls purified and transhumanized. "And it is called Empyrean, which is the same as a heaven blazing with fire or ardor, not because there is in it a natural fire burning, but a spiritual one, which is blessed love or charity."

ELLEN M. MITCHELL

1898.

PARADISO

Canto I

The glory of Him who moveth everything
 Doth penetrate the universe, and shine
 In one part more and in another less.

Within that heaven which most his light receives
 Was I, and things beheld which to repeat
 Nor knows, nor can, who from above descends;

Because in drawing near to its desire
 Our intellect ingulphs itself so far,
 That after it the memory cannot go.

Truly whatever of the holy realm
 I had the power to treasure in my mind
 Shall now become the subject of my song.

O good Apollo, for this last emprise
 Make of me such a vessel of thy power
 As giving the beloved laurel asks!

One summit of Parnassus hitherto
 Has been enough for me, but now with both
 I needs must enter the arena left.

Enter into my bosom, thou, and breathe
 As at the time when Marsyas thou didst draw
 Out of the scabbard of those limbs of his.

O power divine, lend'st thou thyself to me
 So that the shadow of the blessed realm
 Stamped in my brain I can make manifest,

Thou'lt see me come unto thy darling tree,
 And crown myself thereafter with those leaves
 Of which the theme and thou shall make me worthy.

So seldom, Father, do we gather them
 For triumph or of Caesar or of Poet,
 (The fault and shame of human inclinations,)

That the Peneian foliage should bring forth
  Joy to the joyous Delphic deity,
  When any one it makes to thirst for it.

A little spark is followed by great flame;
  Perchance with better voices after me
  Shall prayer be made that Cyrrha may respond!

To mortal men by passages diverse
  Uprises the world's lamp; but by that one
  Which circles four uniteth with three crosses,

With better course and with a better star
  Conjoined it issues, and the mundane wax
  Tempers and stamps more after its own fashion.

Almost that passage had made morning there
  And evening here, and there was wholly white
  That hemisphere, and black the other part,

When Beatrice towards the left-hand side
  I saw turned round, and gazing at the sun;
  Never did eagle fasten so upon it!

And even as a second ray is wont
  To issue from the first and reascend,
  Like to a pilgrim who would fain return,

Thus of her action, through the eyes infused
  In my imagination, mine I made,
  And sunward fixed mine eyes beyond our wont.

There much is lawful which is here unlawful
  Unto our powers, by virtue of the place
  Made for the human species as its own.

Not long I bore it, nor so little while
  But I beheld it sparkle round about
  Like iron that comes molten from the fire;

And suddenly it seemed that day to day
  Was added, as if He who has the power
  Had with another sun the heaven adorned.

With eyes upon the everlasting wheels
  Stood Beatrice all intent, and I, on her
  Fixing my vision from above removed,

Such at her aspect inwardly became
  As Glaucus, tasting of the herb that made him
  Peer of the other gods beneath the sea.

To represent transhumanise in words
  Impossible were; the example, then, suffice
  Him for whom Grace the experience reserves.

If I was merely what of me thou newly
  Createdst, Love who governest the heaven,
  Thou knowest, who didst lift me with thy light!

When now the wheel, which thou dost make eternal
  Desiring thee, made me attentive to it
  By harmony thou dost modulate and measure,

Then seemed to me so much of heaven enkindled
  By the sun's flame, that neither rain nor river
  E'er made a lake so widely spread abroad.

The newness of the sound and the great light
  Kindled in me a longing for their cause,
  Never before with such acuteness felt;

Whence she, who saw me as I saw myself,
  To quiet in me my perturbed mind,
  Opened her mouth, ere I did mine to ask,

And she began: "Thou makest thyself so dull
  With false imagining, that thou seest not
  What thou wouldst see if thou hadst shaken it off.

Thou art not upon earth, as thou believest;
  But lightning, fleeing its appropriate site,
  Ne'er ran as thou, who thitherward returnest."

If of my former doubt I was divested
  By these brief little words more smiled than spoken,
  I in a new one was the more ensnared;

And said: "Already did I rest content
  From great amazement; but am now amazed
  In what way I transcend these bodies light."

Whereupon she, after a pitying sigh,
  Her eyes directed tow'rds me with that look
  A mother casts on a delirious child;

And she began: "All things whate'er they be
  Have order among themselves, and this is form,
  That makes the universe resemble God.

Here do the higher creatures see the footprints
  Of the Eternal Power, which is the end
  Whereto is made the law already mentioned.

In the order that I speak of are inclined
  All natures, by their destinies diverse,
  More or less near unto their origin;

Hence they move onward unto ports diverse
  O'er the great sea of being; and each one
  With instinct given it which bears it on.

This bears away the fire towards the moon;
  This is in mortal hearts the motive power
  This binds together and unites the earth.

Nor only the created things that are
  Without intelligence this bow shoots forth,
  But those that have both intellect and love.

The Providence that regulates all this
  Makes with its light the heaven forever quiet,
  Wherein that turns which has the greatest haste.

And thither now, as to a site decreed,
  Bears us away the virtue of that cord
  Which aims its arrows at a joyous mark.

True is it, that as oftentimes the form
  Accords not with the intention of the art,
  Because in answering is matter deaf,

So likewise from this course doth deviate
  Sometimes the creature, who the power possesses,
  Though thus impelled, to swerve some other way,

(In the same wise as one may see the fire
  Fall from a cloud,) if the first impetus
  Earthward is wrested by some false delight.

Thou shouldst not wonder more, if well I judge,
  At thine ascent, than at a rivulet
  From some high mount descending to the lowland.

Marvel it would be in thee, if deprived
  Of hindrance, thou wert seated down below,
  As if on earth the living fire were quiet."

Thereat she heavenward turned again her face.

Canto II

O Ye, who in some pretty little boat,
  Eager to listen, have been following
  Behind my ship, that singing sails along,

Turn back to look again upon your shores;
  Do not put out to sea, lest peradventure,
  In losing me, you might yourselves be lost.

The sea I sail has never yet been passed;
  Minerva breathes, and pilots me Apollo,
  And Muses nine point out to me the Bears.

Ye other few who have the neck uplifted
  Betimes to th' bread of Angels upon which
  One liveth here and grows not sated by it,

Well may you launch upon the deep salt-sea
  Your vessel, keeping still my wake before you
  Upon the water that grows smooth again.

Those glorious ones who unto Colchos passed
  Were not so wonder-struck as you shall be,
  When Jason they beheld a ploughman made!

The con-created and perpetual thirst
  For the realm deiform did bear us on,
  As swift almost as ye the heavens behold.

Upward gazed Beatrice, and I at her;
  And in such space perchance as strikes a bolt
  And flies, and from the notch unlocks itself,

Arrived I saw me where a wondrous thing
  Drew to itself my sight; and therefore she
  From whom no care of mine could be concealed,

Towards me turning, blithe as beautiful,
  Said unto me: "Fix gratefully thy mind
  On God, who unto the first star has brought us."

It seemed to me a cloud encompassed us,
  Luminous, dense, consolidate and bright
  As adamant on which the sun is striking.

Into itself did the eternal pearl
  Receive us, even as water doth receive
  A ray of light, remaining still unbroken.

If I was body, (and we here conceive not
  How one dimension tolerates another,
  Which needs must be if body enter body,)

More the desire should be enkindled in us
  That essence to behold, wherein is seen
  How God and our own nature were united.

There will be seen what we receive by faith,
  Not demonstrated, but self-evident
  In guise of the first truth that man believes.

I made reply: "Madonna, as devoutly
  As most I can do I give thanks to Him
  Who has removed me from the mortal world.

But tell me what the dusky spots may be
  Upon this body, which below on earth
  Make people tell that fabulous tale of Cain?"

Somewhat she smiled; and then, "If the opinion
  Of mortals be erroneous," she said,
  "Where'er the key of sense doth not unlock,

Certes, the shafts of wonder should not pierce thee
  Now, forasmuch as, following the senses,
  Thou seest that the reason has short wings.

But tell me what thou think'st of it thyself."
  And I: "What seems to us up here diverse,
  Is caused, I think, by bodies rare and dense."

And she: "Right truly shalt thou see immersed
  In error thy belief, if well thou hearest
  The argument that I shall make against it.

Lights many the eighth sphere displays to you
  Which in their quality and quantity
  May noted be of aspects different.

If this were caused by rare and dense alone,
  One only virtue would there be in all
  Or more or less diffused, or equally.

Virtues diverse must be perforce the fruits
  Of formal principles; and these, save one,
  Of course would by thy reasoning be destroyed.

Besides, if rarity were of this dimness
  The cause thou askest, either through and through
  This planet thus attenuate were of matter,

Or else, as in a body is apportioned
  The fat and lean, so in like manner this
  Would in its volume interchange the leaves.

Were it the former, in the sun's eclipse
  It would be manifest by the shining through
  Of light, as through aught tenuous interfused.

This is not so; hence we must scan the other,
  And if it chance the other I demolish,
  Then falsified will thy opinion be.

But if this rarity go not through and through,
  There needs must be a limit, beyond which
  Its contrary prevents the further passing,

And thence the foreign radiance is reflected,
  Even as a color cometh back from glass,
  The which behind itself concealeth lead.

Now thou wilt say the sunbeam shows itself
  More dimly there than in the other parts,
  By being there reflected farther back.

From this reply experiment will free thee
  If e'er thou try it, which is wont to be
  The fountain to the rivers of your arts.

Three mirrors shalt thou take, and two remove
  Alike from thee, the other more remote
  Between the former two shall meet thine eyes.

Turned towards these, cause that behind thy back
  Be placed a light, illuming the three mirrors
  And coming back to thee by all reflected.

Though in its quantity be not so ample
  The image most remote, there shalt thou see
  How it perforce is equally resplendent.

Now, as beneath the touches of warm rays
  Naked the subject of the snow remains
  Both of its former color and its cold,

Thee thus remaining in thy intellect,
  Will I inform with such a living light,
  That it shall tremble in its aspect to thee.

Within the heaven of the divine repose
  Revolves a body, in whose virtue lies
  The being of whatever it contains.

The following heaven, that has so many eyes,
  Divides this being by essences diverse,
  Distinguished from it, and by it contained.

The other spheres, by various differences,
  All the distinctions which they have within them
  Dispose unto their ends and their effects.

Thus do these organs of the world proceed,
  As thou perceivest now, from grade to grade;
  Since from above they take, and act beneath.

Observe me well, how through this place I come
  Unto the truth thou wishest, that hereafter
  Thou mayst alone know how to keep the ford

The power and motion of the holy spheres,
  As from the artisan the hammer's craft,
  Forth from the blessed motors must proceed.

The heaven, which lights so manifold make fair,
  From the Intelligence profound, which turns it,
  The image takes, and makes of it a seal.

And even as the soul within your dust
  Through members different and accommodated
  To faculties diverse expands itself,

So likewise this Intelligence diffuses
  Its virtue multiplied among the stars.
  Itself revolving on its unity.

Virtue diverse doth a diverse alloyage
  Make with the precious body that it quickens,
  In which, as life in you, it is combined.

From the glad nature whence it is derived,
  The mingled virtue through the body shines,
  Even as gladness through the living pupil.

From this proceeds whate'er from light to light
  Appeareth different, not from dense and rare:
  This is the formal principle that produces,

According to its goodness, dark and bright."

Canto III

That Sun, which erst with love my bosom warmed,
  Of beauteous truth had unto me discovered,
  By proving and reproving, the sweet aspect.

And, that I might confess myself convinced
  And confident, so far as was befitting,
  I lifted more erect my head to speak.

But there appeared a vision, which withdrew me
  So close to it, in order to be seen,
  That my confession I remembered not.

Such as through polished and transparent glass,
  Or waters crystalline and undisturbed,
  But not so deep as that their bed be lost,

Come back again the outlines of our faces
  So feeble, that a pearl on forehead white
  Comes not less speedily unto our eyes;

Such saw I many faces prompt to speak,
  So that I ran in error opposite
  To that which kindled love 'twixt man and fountain.

As soon as I became aware of them,
  Esteeming them as mirrored semblances,
  To see of whom they were, mine eyes I turned,

And nothing saw, and once more turned them forward
  Direct into the light of my sweet Guide,
  Who smiling kindled in her holy eyes.

"Marvel thou not," she said to me, "because
  I smile at this thy puerile conceit,
  Since on the truth it trusts not yet its foot,

But turns thee, as 'tis wont, on emptiness.
  True substances are these which thou beholdest,
  Here relegate for breaking of some vow.

Therefore speak with them, listen and believe;
  For the true light, which giveth peace to them,
  Permits them not to turn from it their feet."

And I unto the shade that seemed most wishful
  To speak directed me, and I began,
  As one whom too great eagerness bewilders:

"O well-created spirit, who in the rays
  Of life eternal dost the sweetness taste
  Which being untasted ne'er is comprehended,

Grateful 'twill be to me, if thou content me
  Both with thy name and with your destiny."
  Whereat she promptly and with laughing eyes:

"Our charity doth never shut the doors
  Against a just desire, except as one
  Who wills that all her court be like herself.

I was a virgin sister in the world;
  And if thy mind doth contemplate me well,
  The being more fair will not conceal me from thee,

But thou shalt recognize I am Piccarda,
  Who, stationed here among these other blessed,
  Myself am blessed in the slowest sphere.

All our affections, that alone inflamed
  Are in the pleasure of the Holy Ghost,
  Rejoice at being of his order formed;

And this allotment, which appears so low,
  Therefore is given us, because our vows
  Have been neglected and in some part void."

Whence I to her: "In your miraculous aspects
  There shines I know not what of the divine,
  Which doth transform you from our first conceptions.

Therefore I was not swift in my remembrance;
  But what thou tellest me now aids me so,
  That the refiguring is easier to me.

But tell me, ye who in this place are happy,
  Are you desirous of a higher place,
  To see more or to make yourselves more friends?"

First with those other shades she smiled a little;
  Thereafter answered me so full of gladness,
  She seemed to burn in the first fire of love:

"Brother, our will is quieted by virtue
  Of charity, that makes us wish alone
  For what we have, nor gives us thirst for more.

If to be more exalted we aspired,
  Discordant would our aspirations be
  Unto the will of Him who here secludes us;

Which thou shalt see finds no place in these circles,
  If being in charity is needful here,
  And if thou lookest well into its nature;

Nay, 'tis essential to this blest existence
  To keep itself within the will divine,
  Whereby our very wishes are made one;

So that, as we are station above station
  Throughout this realm, to all the realm 'tis pleasing,
  As to the King, who makes his will our will.

And his will is our peace; this is the sea
  To which is moving onward whatsoever
  It doth create, and all that nature makes."

Then it was clear to me how everywhere
  In heaven is Paradise, although the grace
  Of good supreme there rain not in one measure.

But as it comes to pass, if one food sates,
  And for another still remains the longing,
  We ask for this, and that decline with thanks,

E'en thus did I; with gesture and with word,
  To learn from her what was the web wherein
  She did not ply the shuttle to the end.

"A perfect life and merit high in-heaven
 A lady o'er us," said she, "by whose rule
 Down in your world they vest and veil themselves,

That until death they may both watch and sleep
 Beside that Spouse who every vow accepts
 Which charity conformeth to his pleasure.

To follow her, in girlhood from the world
 I fled, and in her habit shut myself,
 And pledged me to the pathway of her sect.

Then men accustomed unto evil more
 Than unto good, from the sweet cloister tore me;
 God knows what afterward my life became.

This other splendor, which to thee reveals
 Itself on my right side, and is enkindled
 With all the illumination of our sphere,

What of myself I say applies to her;
 A nun was she, and likewise from her head
 Was ta'en the shadow of the sacred wimple.

But when she too was to the world returned
 Against her wishes and against good usage,
 Of the heart's veil she never was divested.

Of great Costanza this is the effulgence,
 Who from the second wind of Suabia
 Brought forth the third and latest puissance."

Thus unto me she spake, and then began
 "Ave Maria" singing, and in singing
 Vanished, as through deep water something heavy.

My sight, that followed her as long a time
 As it was possible, when it had lost her
 Turned round unto the mark of more desire,

And wholly unto Beatrice reverted;
 But she such lightnings flashed into mine eyes,
 That at the first my sight endured it not;

And this in questioning more backward made me.

Canto IV

Between two viands, equally removed
And tempting, a free man would die of hunger
Ere either he could bring unto his teeth.

So would a lamb between the ravenings
Of two fierce wolves stand fearing both alike;
And so would stand a dog between two does.

Hence, if I held my peace, myself I blame not,
Impelled in equal measure by my doubts,
Since it must be so, nor do I commend.

I held my peace; but my desire was painted
Upon my face, and questioning with that
More fervent far than by articulate speech.

Beatrice did as Daniel had done
Relieving Nebuchadnezzar from the wrath
Which rendered him unjustly merciless,

And said: "Well see I how attracteth thee
One and the other wish, so that thy care
Binds itself so that forth it does not breathe.

Thou arguest, if good will be permanent,
The violence of others, for what reason
Doth it decrease the measure of my merit?

Again for doubting furnish thee occasion
Souls seeming to return unto the stars,
According to the sentiment of Plato.

These are the questions which upon thy wish
Are thrusting equally; and therefore first
Will I treat that which hath the most of gall.

He of the Seraphim most absorbed in God,
Moses, and Samuel, and whichever John
Thou mayst select, I say, and even Mary,

Have not in any other heaven their seats,
  Than have those spirits that just appeared to thee,
  Nor of existence more or fewer years;

But all make beautiful the primal circle,
  And have sweet life in different degrees,
  By feeling more or less the eternal breath.

They showed themselves here, not because allotted
  This sphere has been to them, but to give sign
  Of the celestial which is least exalted.

To speak thus is adapted to your mind,
  Since only through the sense it apprehendeth
  What then it worthy makes of intellect.

On this account the Scripture condescends
  Unto your faculties, and feet and hands
  To God attributes, and means something else;

And Holy Church under an aspect human
  Gabriel and Michael represent to you,
  And him who made Tobias whole again.

That which Timaeus argues of the soul
  Doth not resemble that which here is seen,
  Because it seems that as he speaks he thinks.

He says the soul unto its star returns,
  Believing it to have been severed thence
  Whenever nature gave it as a form.

Perhaps his doctrine is of other guise
  Than the words sound, and possibly may be
  With meaning that is not to be derided.

If he doth mean that to these wheels return
  The honor of their influence and the blame,
  Perhaps his bow doth hit upon some truth.

This principle ill understood once warped
  The whole world nearly, till it went astray
  Invoking Jove and Mercury and Mars.

The other doubt which doth disquiet thee
  Less venom has, for its malevolence
  Could never lead thee otherwhere from me.

That as unjust our justice should appear
  In eyes of mortals, is an argument
  Of faith, and not of sin heretical.

But still, that your perception may be able
  To thoroughly penetrate this verity,
  As thou desirest, I will satisfy thee.

If it be violence when he who suffers
  Co-operates not with him who uses force,
  These souls were not on that account excused;

For will is never quenched unless it will,
  But operates as nature doth in fire
  If violence a thousand times distort it.

Hence, if it yieldeth more or less, it seconds
  The force; and these have done so, having power
  Of turning back unto the holy place.

If their will had been perfect, like to that
  Which Lawrence fast upon his gridiron held,
  And Mutius made severe to his own hand,

It would have urged them back along the road
  Whence they were dragged, as soon as they were free;
  But such a solid will is all too rare.

And by these words, if thou hast gathered them
  As thou shouldst do, the argument is refuted
  That would have still annoyed thee many times.

But now another passage runs across
  Before thine eyes, and such that by thyself
  Thou couldst not thread it ere thou wouldst be weary.

I have for certain put into thy mind
  That soul beatified could never lie,
  For it is near the primal Truth,

And then thou from Piccarda might'st have heard
  Costanza kept affection for the veil,
  So that she seemeth here to contradict me.

Many times, brother, has it come to pass,
  That, to escape from peril, with reluctance
  That has been done it was not right to do,

E'en as Alcmaeon (who, being by his father
  Thereto entreated, his own mother slew)
  Not to lose pity pitiless became.

At this point I desire thee to remember
  That force with will commingles, and they cause
  That the offences cannot be excused.

Will absolute consenteth not to evil;
  But in so far consenteth as it fears,
  If it refrain, to fall into more harm.

Hence when Piccarda uses this expression,
  She meaneth the will absolute, and I
  The other, so that both of us speak truth."

Such was the flowing of the holy river
  That issued from the fount whence springs all truth;
  This put to rest my wishes one and all.

"O love of the first lover, O divine,"
  Said I forthwith, "whose speech inundates me
  And warms me so, it more and more revives me,

My own affection is not so profound
  As to suffice in rendering grace for grace;
  Let Him, who sees and can, thereto respond.

Well I perceive that never sated is
  Our intellect unless the Truth illume it,
  Beyond which nothing true expands itself.

It rests therein, as wild beast in his lair,
  When it attains it; and it can attain it;
  If not, then each desire would frustrate be.

Therefore springs up, in fashion of a shoot,
  Doubt at the foot of truth; and this is nature,
  Which to the top from height to height impels us.

This doth invite me, this assurance give me
  With reverence, Lady, to inquire of you
  Another truth, which is obscure to me.

I wish to know if man can satisfy you
  For broken vows with other good deeds, so
  That in your balance they will not be light."

Beatrice gazed upon me with her eyes
  Full of the sparks of love, and so divine,
  That, overcome my power, I turned my back

And almost lost myself with eyes downcast.

Canto V

"If in the heat of love I flame upon thee
  Beyond the measure that on earth is seen,
  So that the valour of thine eyes I vanquish,

Marvel thou not thereat; for this proceeds
  From perfect sight, which as it apprehends
  To the good apprehended moves its feet.

Well I perceive how is already shining
  Into thine intellect the eternal light,
  That only seen enkindles always love;

And if some other thing your love seduce,
  'Tis nothing but a vestige of the same,
  Ill understood, which there is shining through.

Thou fain wouldst know if with another service
  For broken vow can such return be made
  As to secure the soul from further claim."

This Canto thus did Beatrice begin;
  And, as a man who breaks not off his speech,
  Continued thus her holy argument:

"The greatest gift that in his largess God
  Creating made, and unto his own goodness
  Nearest conformed, and that which he doth prize

Most highly, is the freedom of the will,
  Wherewith the creatures of intelligence
  Both all and only were and are endowed.

Now wilt thou see, if thence thou reasonest,
  The high worth of a vow, if it he made
  So that when thou consentest God consents:

For, closing between God and man the compact,
  A sacrifice is of this treasure made,
  Such as I say, and made by its own act.

What can be rendered then as compensation?
  Think'st thou to make good use of what thou'st offered,
  With gains ill gotten thou wouldst do good deed.

Now art thou certain of the greater point;
  But because Holy Church in this dispenses,
  Which seems against the truth which I have shown thee,

Behoves thee still to sit awhile at table,
  Because the solid food which thou hast taken
  Requireth further aid for thy digestion.

Open thy mind to that which I reveal,
  And fix it there within; for 'tis not knowledge,
  The having heard without retaining it.

In the essence of this sacrifice two things
  Convene together; and the one is that
  Of which 'tis made, the other is the agreement.

This last for evermore is cancelled not
  Unless complied with, and concerning this
  With such precision has above been spoken.

Therefore it was enjoined upon the Hebrews
  To offer still, though sometimes what was offered
  Might be commuted, as thou ought'st to know.

The other, which is known to thee as matter,
  May well indeed be such that one errs not
  If it for other matter be exchanged.

But let none shift the burden on his shoulder
  At his arbitrament, without the turning
  Both of the white and of the yellow key;

And every permutation deem as foolish,
  If in the substitute the thing relinquished,
  As the four is in six, be not contained.

Therefore whatever thing has so great weight
  In value that it drags down every balance,
  Cannot be satisfied with other spending.

Let mortals never take a vow in jest;
  Be faithful and not blind in doing that,
  As Jephthah was in his first offering,

Whom more beseemed to say, 'I have done wrong,
  Than to do worse by keeping; and as foolish
  Thou the great leader of the Greeks wilt find,

Whence wept Iphigenia her fair face,
  And made for her both wise and simple weep,
  Who heard such kind of worship spoken of.'

Christians, be ye more serious in your movements;
  Be ye not like a feather at each wind,
  And think not every water washes you.

Ye have the Old and the New Testament,
  And the Pastor of the Church who guideth you
  Let this suffice you unto your salvation.

If evil appetite cry aught else to you,
  Be ye as men, and not as silly sheep,
  So that the Jew among you may not mock you.

Be ye not as the lamb that doth abandon
  Its mother's milk, and frolicsome and simple
  Combats at its own pleasure with itself."

Thus Beatrice to me even as I write it;
  Then all desireful turned herself again
  To that part where the world is most alive.

Her silence and her change of countenance
  Silence imposed upon my eager mind,
  That had already in advance new questions;

And as an arrow that upon the mark
  Strikes ere the bowstring quiet hath become,
  So did we speed into the second realm.

My Lady there so joyful I beheld,
  As into the brightness of that heaven she entered,
  More luminous thereat the planet grew;

And if the star itself was changed and smiled,
  What became I, who by my nature am
  Exceeding mutable in every guise!

As, in a fish-pond which is pure and tranquil,
  The fishes draw to that which from without
  Comes in such fashion that their food they deem it;

So I beheld more than a thousand splendors
  Drawing towards us, and in each was heard:
  "Lo, this is she who shall increase our love."

And as each one was coming unto us,
  Full of beatitude the shade was seen,
  By the effulgence clear that issued from it.

Think, Reader, if what here is just beginning
  No farther should proceed, how thou wouldst have
  An agonizing need of knowing more;

And of thyself thou'lt see how I from these
  Was in desire of hearing their conditions,
  As they unto mine eyes were manifest.

"O thou well-born, unto whom Grace concedes
  To see the thrones of the eternal triumph,
  Or ever yet the warfare be abandoned

With light that through the whole of heaven is spread
  Kindled are we, and hence if thou desirest
  To know of us, at thine own pleasure sate thee."

Thus by some one among those holy spirits
  Was spoken, and by Beatrice: "Speak, speak
  Securely, and believe them even as Gods."

"Well I perceive how thou dost nest thyself
  In thine own light, and drawest it from thine eyes,
  Because they coruscate when thou dost smile,

But know not who thou art, nor why thou hast,
  Spirit august, thy station in the sphere
  That veils itself to men in alien rays."

This said I in direction of the light
  Which first had spoken to me; whence it became
  By far more lucent than it was before.

Even as the sun, that doth conceal himself
  By too much light, when heat has worn away
  The tempering influence of the vapours dense,

By greater rapture thus concealed itself
  In its own radiance the figure saintly,
  And thus close, close enfolded answered me

In fashion as the following Canto sings.

Canto VI

"After that Constantine the eagle turned
  Against the course of heaven, which it had followed
  Behind the ancient who Lavinia took,

Two hundred years and more the bird of God
  In the extreme of Europe held itself,
  Near to the mountains whence it issued first;

And under shadow of the sacred plumes
  It governed there the world from hand to hand,
  And, changing thus, upon mine own alighted.

Caesar I was, and am Justinian,
  Who, by the will of primal Love I feel,
  Took from the laws the useless and redundant;

And ere unto the work I was attent,
  One nature to exist in Christ, not more,
  Believed, and with such faith was I contented.

But blessed Agapetus, he who was
  The supreme pastor, to the faith sincere
  Pointed me out the way by words of his.

Him I believed, and what was his assertion
  I now see clearly, even as thou seest
  Each contradiction to be false and true.

As soon as with the Church I moved my feet,
  God in his grace it pleased with this high task
  To inspire me, and I gave me wholly to it,

And to my Belisarius I commended
  The arms, to which was heaven's right hand so joined
  It was a signal that I should repose.

Now here to the first question terminates
  My answer; but the character thereof
  Constrains me to continue with a sequel,

In order that thou see with how great reason
  Men move against the standard sacrosanct,
  Both who appropriate and who oppose it.

Behold how great a power has made it worthy
  Of reverence, beginning from the hour
  When Pallas died to give it sovereignty.

Thou knowest it made in Alba its abode
  Three hundred years and upward, till at last
  The three to three fought for it yet again.

Thou knowest what it achieved from Sabine wrong
  Down to Lucretia's sorrow, in seven kings
  O'ercoming round about the neighboring nations;

Thou knowest what it achieved, borne by the Romans
  Illustrious against Brennus, against Pyrrhus,
  Against the other princes and confederates.

Torquatus thence and Quinctius, who from locks
  Unkempt was named, Decii and Fabii,
  Received the fame I willingly embalm;

It struck to earth the pride of the Arabians,
  Who, following Hannibal, had passed across
  The Alpine ridges, Po, from which thou glidest;

Beneath it triumphed while they yet were young
  Pompey and Scipio, and to the hill
  Beneath which thou wast born it bitter seemed;

Then, near unto the time when heaven had willed
  To bring the whole world to its mood serene,
  Did Caesar by the will of Rome assume it.

What it achieved from Var unto the Rhine,
  Isere beheld and Saone, beheld the Seine,
  And every valley whence the Rhone is filled;

What it achieved when it had left Ravenna,
  And leaped the Rubicon, was such a flight
  That neither tongue nor pen could follow it.

Round towards Spain it wheeled its legions; then
  Towards Durazzo, and Pharsalia smote
  That to the calid Nile was felt the pain.

Antandros and the Simois, whence it started,
  It saw again, and there where Hector lies,
  And ill for Ptolemy then roused itself.

From thence it came like lightning upon Juba;
  Then wheeled itself again into your West,
  Where the Pompeian clarion it heard.

From what it wrought with the next standard-bearer
  Brutus and Cassius howl in Hell together,
  And Modena and Perugia dolent were;

Still doth the mournful Cleopatra weep
  Because thereof, who, fleeing from before it,
  Took from the adder sudden and black death.

With him it ran even to the Red Sea shore;
  With him it placed the world in so great peace,
  That unto Janus was his temple closed.

But what the standard that has made me speak
  Achieved before, and after should achieve
  Throughout the mortal realm that lies beneath it,

Becometh in appearance mean and dim,
  If in the hand of the third Caesar seen
  With eye unclouded and affection pure,

Because the living Justice that inspires me
  Granted it, in the hand of him I speak of,
  The glory of doing vengeance for its wrath.

Now here attend to what I answer thee;
  Later it ran with Titus to do vengeance
  Upon the vengeance of the ancient sin.

And when the tooth of Lombardy had bitten
  The Holy Church, then underneath its wings
  Did Charlemagne victorious succor her.

Now hast thou power to judge of such as those
  Whom I accused above, and of their crimes,
  Which are the cause of all your miseries.

To the public standard one the yellow lilies
  Opposes, the other claims it for a party,
  So that 'tis hard to see which sins the most.

Let, let the Ghibellines ply their handicraft
  Beneath some other standard; for this ever
  Ill follows he who it and justice parts.

And let not this new Charles e'er strike it down,
  He and his Guelfs, but let him fear the talons
  That from a nobler lion stripped the fell.

Already oftentimes the sons have wept
  The father's crime; and let him not believe
  That God will change His scutcheon for the lilies.

This little planet doth adorn itself
  With the good spirits that have active been,
  That fame and honor might come after them;

And whensoever the desires mount thither,
  Thus deviating, must perforce the rays
  Of the true love less vividly mount upward.

But in commensuration of our wages
  With our desert is portion of our joy,
  Because we see them neither less nor greater.

Herein doth living Justice sweeten so
  Affection in us, that for evermore
  It cannot warp to any iniquity.

Voices diverse make up sweet melodies;
  So in this life of ours the seats diverse
  Render sweet harmony among these spheres;

And in the compass of this present pearl
  Shineth the sheen of Romeo, of whom
  The grand and beauteous work was ill rewarded.

But the Provencals who against him wrought,
  They have not laughed, and therefore ill goes he
  Who makes his hurt of the good deeds of others.

Four daughters, and each one of them a queen,
  Had Raymond Berenger, and this for him
  Did Romeo, a poor man and a pilgrim;

And then malicious words incited him
  To summon to a reckoning this just man,
  Who rendered to him seven and five for ten.

Then he departed poor and stricken in years,
  And if the world could know the heart he had,
  In begging bit by bit his livelihood,

Though much it laud him, it would laud him more."

Canto VII

"Osanna sanctus Deus Sabaoth,
  Superillustrans claritate tua
  Felices ignes horum malahoth!"

In this wise, to his melody returning,
  This substance, upon which a double light
  Doubles itself, was seen by me to sing,

And to their dance this and the others moved,
  And in the manner of swift-hurrying sparks
  Veiled themselves from me with a sudden distance.

Doubting was I, and saying, "Tell her, tell her,"
  Within me, "tell her," saying, "tell my Lady,"
  Who slakes my thirst with her sweet effluences;

And yet that reverence which doth lord it over
  The whole of me only by B and ICE,
  Bowed me again like unto one who drowses.

Short while did Beatrice endure me thus;
  And she began, lighting me with a smile
  Such as would make one happy in the fire:

"According to infallible advisement,
  After what manner a just vengeance justly
  Could be avenged has put thee upon thinking,

But I will speedily thy mind unloose;
  And do thou listen, for these words of mine
  Of a great doctrine will a present make thee.

By not enduring on the power that wills
  Curb for his good, that man who ne'er was born,
  Damning himself damned all his progeny;

Whereby the human species down below
  Lay sick for many centuries in great error,
  Till to descend it pleased the Word of God

To where the nature, which from its own Maker
  Estranged itself, he joined to him in person
  By the sole act of his eternal love.

Now unto what is said direct thy sight;
  This nature when united to its Maker,
  Such as created, was sincere and good;

But by itself alone was banished forth
  From Paradise, because it turned aside
  Out of the way of truth and of its life.

Therefore the penalty the cross held out,
  If measured by the nature thus assumed,
  None ever yet with so great justice stung,

And none was ever of so great injustice,
  Considering who the Person was that suffered,
  Within whom such a nature was contracted.

From one act therefore issued things diverse;
  To God and to the Jews one death was pleasing;
  Earth trembled at it and the Heaven was opened.

It should no longer now seem difficult
  To thee, when it is said that a just vengeance
  By a just court was afterward avenged.

But now do I behold thy mind entangled
  From thought to thought within a knot, from which
  With great desire it waits to free itself.

Thou sayest, 'Well discern I what I hear;
  But it is hidden from me why God willed
  For our redemption only this one mode.'

Buried remaineth, brother, this decree
  Unto the eyes of every one whose nature
  Is in the flame of love not yet adult.

Verily, inasmuch as at this mark
  One gazes long and little is discerned,
  Wherefore this mode was worthiest will I say.

Goodness Divine, which from itself doth spurn
  All envy, burning in itself so sparkles
  That the eternal beauties it unfolds.

Whate'er from this immediately distils
  Has afterwards no end, for ne'er removed
  Is its impression when it sets its seal.

Whate'er from this immediately rains down
  Is wholly free, because it is not subject
  Unto the influences of novel things.

The more conformed thereto, the more it pleases;
  For the blest ardour that irradiates all things
  In that most like itself is most vivacious.

With all of these things has advantaged been
  The human creature; and if one be wanting,
  From his nobility he needs must fall.

'Tis sin alone which doth disfranchise him,
  And render him unlike the Good Supreme,
  So that he little with its light is blanched,

And to his dignity no more returns,
  Unless he fill up where transgression empties
  With righteous pains for criminal delights.

Your nature when it sinned so utterly
  In its own seed, out of these dignities
  Even as out of Paradise was driven,

Nor could itself recover, if thou notest
  With nicest subtilty, by any way,
  Except by passing one of these two fords:

Either that God through clemency alone
  Had pardon granted, or that man himself
  Had satisfaction for his folly made.

Fix now thine eye deep into the abyss
  Of the eternal counsel, to my speech
  As far as may be fastened steadfastly!

Man in his limitations had not power
  To satisfy, not having power to sink
  In his humility obeying then,

Far as he disobeying thought to rise;
  And for this reason man has been from power
  Of satisfying by himself excluded.

Therefore it God behoved in his own ways
  Man to restore unto his perfect life,
  I say in one, or else in both of them.

But since the action of the doer is
  So much more grateful, as it more presents
  The goodness of the heart from which it issues,

Goodness Divine, that doth imprint the world,
  Has been contented to proceed by each
  And all its ways to lift you up again;

Nor 'twixt the first day and the final night
  Such high and such magnificent proceeding
  By one or by the other was or shall be;

For God more bounteous was himself to give
  To make man able to uplift himself,
  Than if he only of himself had pardoned;

And all the other modes were insufficient
  For justice, were it not the Son of God
  Himself had humbled to become incarnate.

Now, to fill fully each desire of thine,
  Return I to elucidate one place,
  In order that thou there mayst see as I do.

Thou sayst: 'I see the air, I see the fire,
  The water, and the earth, and all their mixtures
  Come to corruption, and short while endure;

And these things notwithstanding were created;'
  Therefore if that which I have said were true,
  They should have been secure against corruption.

The Angels, brother, and the land sincere
  In which thou art, created may be called
  Just as they are in their entire existence;

But all the elements which thou hast named,
  And all those things which out of them are made,
  By a created virtue are informed.

Created was the matter which they have;
  Created was the informing influence
  Within these stars that round about them go.

The soul of every brute and of the plants
  By its potential temperament attracts
  The ray and motion of the holy lights;

But your own life immediately inspires
  Supreme Beneficence, and enamours it
  So with herself, it evermore desires her.

And thou from this mayst argue furthermore
  Your resurrection, if thou think again
  How human flesh was fashioned at that time

When the first parents both of them were made."

Canto VIII

The world used in its peril to believe
  That the fair Cypria delirious love
  Rayed out, in the third epicycle turning;

Wherefore not only unto her paid honor
  Of sacrifices and of votive cry
  The ancient nations in the ancient error,

But both Dione honored they and Cupid,
  That as her mother, this one as her son,
  And said that he had sat in Dido's lap;

And they from her, whence I beginning take,
  Took the denomination of the star
  That woos the sun, now following, now in front.

I was not ware of our ascending to it;
  But of our being in it gave full faith
  My Lady whom I saw more beauteous grow.

And as within a flame a spark is seen,
  And as within a voice a voice discerned,
  When one is steadfast, and one comes and goes,

Within that light beheld I other lamps
  Move in a circle, speeding more and less,
  Methinks in measure of their inward vision.

From a cold cloud descended never winds,
  Or visible or not, so rapidly
  They would not laggard and impeded seem

To any one who had those lights divine
  Seen come towards us, leaving the gyration
  Begun at first in the high Seraphim.

And behind those that most in front appeared
  Sounded "Osanna!" so that never since
  To hear again was I without desire.

Then unto us more nearly one approached,
  And it alone began: "We all are ready
  Unto thy pleasure, that thou joy in us.

We turn around with the celestial Princes,
  One gyre and one gyration and one thirst,
  To whom thou in the world of old didst say,

'Ye who, intelligent, the third heaven are moving;'
  And are so full of love, to pleasure thee
  A little quiet will not be less sweet."

After these eyes of mine themselves had offered
  Unto my Lady reverently, and she
  Content and certain of herself had made them,

Back to the light they turned, which so great promise
  Made of itself, and "Say, who art thou?" was
  My voice, imprinted with a great affection.

O how and how much I beheld it grow
  With the new joy that superadded was
  Unto its joys, as soon as I had spoken!

Thus changed, it said to me: "The world possessed me
  Short time below; and, if it had been more,
  Much evil will be which would not have been.

My gladness keepeth me concealed from thee,
  Which rayeth round about me, and doth hide me
  Like as a creature swathed in its own silk.

Much didst thou love me, and thou hadst good reason;
  For had I been below, I should have shown thee
  Somewhat beyond the foliage of my love.

That left-hand margin, which doth bathe itself
  In Rhone, when it is mingled with the Sorgue,
  Me for its lord awaited in due time,

And that horn of Ausonia, which is towned
  With Bari, with Gaeta and Catona,
  Whence Tronto and Verde in the sea disgorge.

Already flashed upon my brow the crown
  Of that dominion which the Danube waters
  After the German borders it abandons;

And beautiful Trinacria, that is murky
  'Twixt Pachino and Peloro, (on the gulf
  Which greatest scath from Eurus doth receive,)

Not through Typhoeus, but through nascent sulphur,
  Would have awaited her own monarchs still,
  Through me from Charles descended and from Rudolph,

If evil lordship, that exasperates ever
  The subject populations, had not moved
  Palermo to the outcry of 'Death! death!'

And if my brother could but this foresee,
  The greedy poverty of Catalonia
  Straight would he flee, that it might not molest him;

For verily 'tis needful to provide,
  Through him or other, so that on his bark
  Already freighted no more freight be placed.

His nature, which from liberal covetous
  Descended, such a soldiery would need
  As should not care for hoarding in a chest."

"Because I do believe the lofty joy
  Thy speech infuses into me, my Lord,
  Where every good thing doth begin and end

Thou seest as I see it, the more grateful
  Is it to me; and this too hold I dear,
  That gazing upon God thou dost discern it.

Glad hast thou made me; so make clear to me,
  Since speaking thou hast stirred me up to doubt,
  How from sweet seed can bitter issue forth."

This I to him; and he to me: "If I
  Can show to thee a truth, to what thou askest
  Thy face thou'lt hold as thou dost hold thy back.

The Good which all the realm thou art ascending
  Turns and contents, maketh its providence
  To be a power within these bodies vast;

And not alone the natures are foreseen
  Within the mind that in itself is perfect,
  But they together with their preservation.

For whatsoever thing this bow shoots forth
  Falls foreordained unto an end foreseen,
  Even as a shaft directed to its mark.

If that were not, the heaven which thou dost walk
  Would in such manner its effects produce,
  That they no longer would be arts, but ruins.

This cannot be, if the Intelligences
  That keep these stars in motion are not maimed,
  And maimed the First that has not made them perfect.

Wilt thou this truth have clearer made to thee?"
  And I: "Not so; for 'tis impossible
  That nature tire, I see, in what is needful."

Whence he again: "Now say, would it be worse
  For men on earth were they not citizens?"
  "Yes," I replied; "and here I ask no reason."

"And can they be so, if below they live not
  Diversely unto offices diverse?
  No, if your master writeth well for you."

So came he with deductions to this point;
  Then he concluded: "Therefore it behoves
  The roots of your effects to be diverse.

Hence one is Solon born, another Xerxes,
  Another Melchisedec, and another he
  Who, flying through the air, his son did lose.

Revolving Nature, which a signet is
  To mortal wax, doth practise well her art,
  But not one inn distinguish from another;

Thence happens it that Esau differeth
  In seed from Jacob; and Quirinus comes
  From sire so vile that he is given to Mars.

A generated nature its own way
  Would always make like its progenitors,
  If Providence divine were not triumphant.

Now that which was behind thee is before thee;
  But that thou know that I with thee am pleased,
  With a corollary will I mantle thee.

Evermore nature, if it fortune find
  Discordant to it, like each other seed
  Out of its region, maketh evil thrift;

And if the world below would fix its mind
  On the foundation which is laid by nature,
  Pursuing that, 'twould have the people good.

But you unto religion wrench aside
　Him who was born to gird him with the sword,
　And make a king of him who is for sermons;

Therefore your footsteps wander from the road."

Canto IX

Beautiful Clemence, after that thy Charles
　Had me enlightened, he narrated to me
　The treacheries his seed should undergo;

But said: "Be still and let the years roll round;"
　So I can only say, that lamentation
　Legitimate shall follow on your wrongs.

And of that holy light the life already
　Had to the Sun which fills it turned again,
　As to that good which for each thing sufficeth.

Ah, souls deceived, and creatures impious,
　Who from such good do turn away your hearts,
　Directing upon vanity your foreheads!

And now, behold, another of those splendors
　Approached me, and its will to pleasure me
　It signified by brightening outwardly.

The eyes of Beatrice, that fastened were
　Upon me, as before, of dear assent
　To my desire assurance gave to me.

"Ah, bring swift compensation to my wish,
　Thou blessed spirit," I said, "and give me proof
　That what I think in thee I can reflect!"

Whereat the light, that still was new to me,
　Out of its depths, whence it before was singing,
　As one delighted to do good, continued:

"Within that region of the land depraved
　Of Italy, that lies between Rialto
　And fountain-heads of Brenta and of Piava,

Rises a hill, and mounts not very high,
  Wherefrom descended formerly a torch
  That made upon that region great assault.

Out of one root were born both I and it;
  Cunizza was I called, and here I shine
  Because the splendor of this star o'ercame me.

But gladly to myself the cause I pardon
  Of my allotment, and it does not grieve me;
  Which would perhaps seem strong unto your vulgar.

Of this so luculent and precious jewel,
  Which of our heaven is nearest unto me,
  Great fame remained; and ere it die away

This hundredth year shall yet quintupled be.
  See if man ought to make him excellent,
  So that another life the first may leave!

And thus thinks not the present multitude
  Shut in by Adige and Tagliamento,
  Nor yet for being scourged is penitent.

But soon 'twill be that Padua in the marsh
  Will change the water that Vicenza bathes,
  Because the folk are stubborn against duty;

And where the Sile and Cagnano join
  One lordeth it, and goes with lofty head,
  For catching whom e'en now the net is making.

Feltro moreover of her impious pastor
  Shall weep the crime, which shall so monstrous be
  That for the like none ever entered Malta.

Ample exceedingly would be the vat
  That of the Ferrarese could hold the blood,
  And weary who should weigh it ounce by ounce,

Of which this courteous priest shall make a gift
  To show himself a partisan; and such gifts
  Will to the living of the land conform.

Above us there are mirrors, Thrones you call them,
  From which shines out on us God Judicant,
  So that this utterance seems good to us."

Here it was silent, and it had the semblance
  Of being turned elsewhither, by the wheel
  On which it entered as it was before.

The other joy, already known to me,
  Became a thing transplendent in my sight,
  As a fine ruby smitten by the sun.

Through joy effulgence is acquired above,
  As here a smile; but down below, the shade
  Outwardly darkens, as the mind is sad.

"God seeth all things, and in Him, blest spirit,
  Thy sight is," said I, "so that never will
  Of his can possibly from thee be hidden;

Thy voice, then, that for ever makes the heavens
  Glad, with the singing of those holy fires
  Which of their six wings make themselves a cowl,

Wherefore does it not satisfy my longings?
  Indeed, I would not wait thy questioning
  If I in thee were as thou art in me."

"The greatest of the valleys where the water
  Expands itself," forthwith its words began,
  "That sea excepted which the earth engarlands,

Between discordant shores against the sun
  Extends so far, that it meridian makes
  Where it was wont before to make the horizon.

I was a dweller on that valley's shore
  'Twixt Ebro and Magra that with journey short
  Doth from the Tuscan part the Genoese.

With the same sunset and same sunrise nearly
  Sit Buggia and the city whence I was,
  That with its blood once made the harbour hot.

Folco that people called me unto whom
  My name was known; and now with me this heaven
  Imprints itself, as I did once with it;

For more the daughter of Belus never burned,
  Offending both Sichaeus and Creusa,
  Than I, so long as it became my locks,

Nor yet that Rodophean, who deluded
  was by Demophoon, nor yet Alcides,
  When Iole he in his heart had locked.

Yet here is no repenting, but we smile,
  Not at the fault, which comes not back to mind,
  But at the power which ordered and foresaw.

Here we behold the art that doth adorn
  With such affection, and the good discover
  Whereby the world above turns that below.

But that thou wholly satisfied mayst bear
  Thy wishes hence which in this sphere are born,
  Still farther to proceed behoveth me.

Thou fain wouldst know who is within this light
  That here beside me thus is scintillating,
  Even as a sunbeam in the limpid water.

Then know thou, that within there is at rest
  Rahab, and being to our order joined,
  With her in its supremest grade 'tis sealed.

Into this heaven, where ends the shadowy cone
  Cast by your world, before all other souls
  First of Christ's triumph was she taken up.

Full meet it was to leave her in some heaven,
  Even as a palm of the high victory
  Which he acquired with one palm and the other,

Because she favoured the first glorious deed
  Of Joshua upon the Holy Land,
  That little stirs the memory of the Pope.

Thy city, which an offshoot is of him
  Who first upon his Maker turned his back,
  And whose ambition is so sorely wept,

Brings forth and scatters the accursed flower
  Which both the sheep and lambs hath led astray
  Since it has turned the shepherd to a wolf.

For this the Evangel and the mighty Doctors
  Are derelict, and only the Decretals
  So studied that it shows upon their margins.

On this are Pope and Cardinals intent;
  Their meditations reach not Nazareth,
  There where his pinions Gabriel unfolded;

But Vatican and the other parts elect
  Of Rome, which have a cemetery been
  Unto the soldiery that followed Peter

Shall soon be free from this adultery."

Canto X

Looking into his Son with all the Love
  Which each of them eternally breathes forth,
  The Primal and unutterable Power

Whate'er before the mind or eye revolves
  With so much order made, there can be none
  Who this beholds without enjoying Him.

Lift up then, Reader, to the lofty wheels
  With me thy vision straight unto that part
  Where the one motion on the other strikes,

And there begin to contemplate with joy
  That Master's art, who in himself so loves it
  That never doth his eye depart therefrom.

Behold how from that point goes branching off
  The oblique circle, which conveys the planets,
  To satisfy the world that calls upon them;

And if their pathway were not thus inflected,
  Much virtue in the heavens would be in vain,
  And almost every power below here dead.

If from the straight line distant more or less
  Were the departure, much would wanting be
  Above and underneath of mundane order.

Remain now, Reader, still upon thy bench,
  In thought pursuing that which is foretasted,
  If thou wouldst jocund be instead of weary.

I've set before thee; henceforth feed thyself,
  For to itself diverteth all my care
  That theme whereof I have been made the scribe.

The greatest of the ministers of nature,
  Who with the power of heaven the world imprints
  And measures with his light the time for us,

With that part which above is called to mind
  Conjoined, along the spirals was revolving,
  Where each time earlier he presents himself;

And I was with him; but of the ascending
  I was not conscious, saving as a man
  Of a first thought is conscious ere it come;

And Beatrice, she who is seen to pass
  From good to better, and so suddenly
  That not by time her action is expressed,

How lucent in herself must she have been!
  And what was in the sun, wherein I entered,
  Apparent not by color but by light,

I, though I call on genius, art, and practice,
  Cannot so tell that it could be imagined;
  Believe one can, and let him long to see it.

And if our fantasies too lowly are
  For altitude so great, it is no marvel,
  Since o'er the sun was never eye could go.

Such in this place was the fourth family
  Of the high Father, who forever sates it,
  Showing how he breathes forth and how begets.

And Beatrice began: "Give thanks, give thanks
  Unto the Sun of Angels, who to this
  Sensible one has raised thee by his grace!"

Never was heart of mortal so disposed
  To worship, nor to give itself to God
  With all its gratitude was it so ready,

As at those words did I myself become;
  And all my love was so absorbed in Him,
  That in oblivion Beatrice was eclipsed.

Nor this displeased her; but she smiled at it
  So that the splendor of her laughing eyes
  My single mind on many things divided.

Lights many saw I, vivid and triumphant,
  Make us a centre and themselves a circle,
  More sweet in voice than luminous in aspect.

Thus girt about the daughter of Latona
  We sometimes see, when pregnant is the air,
  So that it holds the thread which makes her zone.

Within the court of Heaven, whence I return,
  Are many jewels found, so fair and precious
  They cannot be transported from the realm;

And of them was the singing of those lights.
  Who takes not wings that he may fly up thither,
  The tidings thence may from the dumb await!

As soon as singing thus those burning suns
  Had round about us whirled themselves three times,
  Like unto stars neighboring the steadfast poles,

Ladies they seemed, not from the dance released,
  But who stop short, in silence listening
  Till they have gathered the new melody.

And within one I heard beginning: "When
  The radiance of grace, by which is kindled
  True love, and which thereafter grows by loving,

Within thee multiplied is so resplendent
  That it conducts thee upward by that stair,
  Where without reascending none descends,

Who should deny the wine out of his vial
  Unto thy thirst, in liberty were not
  Except as water which descends not seaward.

Fain wouldst thou know with what plants is enflowered
  This garland that encircles with delight
  The Lady fair who makes thee strong for heaven.

Of the lambs was I of the holy flock
  Which Dominic conducteth by a road
  Where well one fattens if he strayeth not.

He who is nearest to me on the right
  My brother and master was; and he Albertus
  Is of Cologne, I Thomas of Aquinum.

If thou of all the others wouldst be certain,
  Follow behind my speaking with thy sight
  Upward along the blessed garland turning.

That next effulgence issues from the smile
  Of Gratian, who assisted both the courts
  In such wise that it pleased in Paradise.

The other which near by adorns our choir
  That Peter was who, e'en as the poor widow,
  Offered his treasure unto Holy Church.

The fifth light, that among us is the fairest,
  Breathes forth from such a love, that all the world
  Below is greedy to learn tidings of it.

Within it is the lofty mind, where knowledge
  So deep was put, that, if the true be true,
  To see so much there never rose a second.

Thou seest next the lustre of that taper,
  Which in the flesh below looked most within
  The angelic nature and its ministry.

Within that other little light is smiling
  The advocate of the Christian centuries,
  Out of whose rhetoric Augustine was furnished.

Now if thou trainest thy mind's eye along
  From light to light pursuant of my praise,
  With thirst already of the eighth thou waitest.

By seeing every good therein exults
  The sainted soul, which the fallacious world
  Makes manifest to him who listeneth well;

The body whence 'twas hunted forth is lying
  Down in Cieldauro, and from martyrdom
  And banishment it came unto this peace.

See farther onward flame the burning breath
  Of Isidore, of Beda, and of Richard
  Who was in contemplation more than man.

This, whence to me returneth thy regard,
  The light is of a spirit unto whom
  In his grave meditations death seemed slow.

It is the light eternal of Sigier,
  Who, reading lectures in the Street of Straw,
  Did syllogize invidious verities."

Then, as a horologe that calleth us
  What time the Bride of God is rising up
  With matins to her Spouse that he may love her,

Wherein one part the other draws and urges,
  Ting! ting! resounding with so sweet a note,
  That swells with love the spirit well disposed,

Thus I beheld the glorious wheel move round,
  And render voice to voice, in modulation
  And sweetness that can not be comprehended,

Excepting there where joy is made eternal.

Canto XI

O Thou insensate care of mortal men,
  How inconclusive are the syllogisms
  That make thee beat thy wings in downward flight!

One after laws and one to aphorisms
  Was going, and one following the priesthood,
  And one to reign by force or sophistry,

And one in theft, and one in state affairs,
  One in the pleasures of the flesh involved
  Wearied himself, one gave himself to ease;

When I, from all these things emancipate,
  With Beatrice above there in the Heavens
  With such exceeding glory was received!

When each one had returned unto that point
  Within the circle where it was before,
  It stood as in a candlestick a candle;

And from within the effulgence which at first
  Had spoken unto me, I heard begin
  Smiling while it more luminous became:

"Even as I am kindled in its ray,
  So, looking into the Eternal Light,
  The occasion of thy thoughts I apprehend.

Thou doubtest, and wouldst have me to resift
  In language so extended and so open
  My speech, that to thy sense it may be plain,

Where just before I said, 'where well one fattens,'
  And where I said, 'there never rose a second;'
  And here 'tis needful we distinguish well.

The Providence, which governeth the world
  With counsel, wherein all created vision
  Is vanquished ere it reach unto the bottom,

(So that towards her own Beloved might go
  The bride of Him who, uttering a loud cry,
  Espoused her with his consecrated blood,

Self-confident and unto Him more faithful,)
  Two Princes did ordain in her behoof,
  Which on this side and that might be her guide.

The one was all seraphical in ardour;
  The other by his wisdom upon earth
  A splendor was of light cherubical.

One will I speak of, for of both is spoken
  In praising one, whichever may be taken,
  Because unto one end their labours were.

Between Tupino and the stream that falls
  Down from the hill elect of blessed Ubald,
  A fertile slope of lofty mountain hangs,

From which Perugia feels the cold and heat
  Through Porta Sole, and behind it weep
  Gualdo and Nocera their grievous yoke.

From out that slope, there where it breaketh most
  Its steepness, rose upon the world a sun
  As this one does sometimes from out the Ganges;

Therefore let him who speaketh of that place,
  Say not Ascesi, for he would say little,
  But Orient, if he properly would speak.

He was not yet far distant from his rising
  Before he had begun to make the earth
  Some comfort from his mighty virtue feel.

For he in youth his father's wrath incurred
  For certain Dame, to whom, as unto death,
  The gate of pleasure no one doth unlock;

And was before his spiritual court
  'Et coram patre' unto her united;
  Then day by day more fervently he loved her.

She, reft of her first husband, scorned, obscure,
  One thousand and one hundred years and more,
  Waited without a suitor till he came.

Naught it availed to hear, that with Amyclas
  Found her unmoved at sounding of his voice
  He who struck terror into all the world;

Naught it availed being constant and undaunted,
  So that, when Mary still remained below,
  She mounted up with Christ upon the cross.

But that too darkly I may not proceed,
  Francis and Poverty for these two lovers
  Take thou henceforward in my speech diffuse.

Their concord and their joyous semblances,
  The love, the wonder, and the sweet regard,
  They made to be the cause of holy thoughts;

So much so that the venerable Bernard
  First bared his feet, and after so great peace
  Ran, and, in running, thought himself too slow.

O wealth unknown! O veritable good!
  Giles bares his feet, and bares his feet Sylvester
  Behind the bridegroom, so doth please the bride!

Then goes his way that father and that master,
  He and his Lady and that family
  Which now was girding on the humble cord;

Nor cowardice of heart weighed down his brow
  At being son of Peter Bernardone,
  Nor for appearing marvellously scorned;

But regally his hard determination
  To Innocent he opened, and from him
  Received the primal seal upon his Order.

After the people mendicant increased
  Behind this man, whose admirable life
  Better in glory of the heavens were sung,

Incoronated with a second crown
  Was through Honorius by the Eternal Spirit
  The holy purpose of this Archimandrite.

And when he had, through thirst of martyrdom,
  In the proud presence of the Sultan preached
  Christ and the others who came after him,

And, finding for conversion too unripe
  The folk, and not to tarry there in vain,
  Returned to fruit of the Italic grass,

On the rude rock 'twixt Tiber and the Arno
  From Christ did he receive the final seal,
  Which during two whole years his members bore.

When He, who chose him unto so much good,
  Was pleased to draw him up to the reward
  That he had merited by being lowly,

Unto his friars, as to the rightful heirs,
  His most dear Lady did he recommend,
  And bade that they should love her faithfully;

And from her bosom the illustrious soul
  Wished to depart, returning to its realm,
  And for its body wished no other bier.

Think now what man was he, who was a fit
  Companion over the high seas to keep
  The bark of Peter to its proper bearings.

And this man was our Patriarch; hence whoever
  Doth follow him as he commands can see
  That he is laden with good merchandise.

But for new pasturage his flock has grown
  So greedy, that it is impossible
  They be not scattered over fields diverse;

And in proportion as his sheep remote
  And vagabond go farther off from him,
  More void of milk return they to the fold.

Verily some there are that fear a hurt,
  And keep close to the shepherd; but so few,
  That little cloth doth furnish forth their hoods.

Now if my utterance be not indistinct,
  If thine own hearing hath attentive been,
  If thou recall to mind what I have said,

In part contented shall thy wishes be;
  For thou shalt see the plant that's chipped away,
  And the rebuke that lieth in the words,

'Where well one fattens, if he strayeth not.'"

Canto XII

Soon as the blessed flame had taken up
  The final word to give it utterance,
  Began the holy millstone to revolve,

And in its gyre had not turned wholly round,
  Before another in a ring enclosed it,
  And motion joined to motion, song to song;

Song that as greatly doth transcend our Muses,
  Our Sirens, in those dulcet clarions,
  As primal splendor that which is reflected.

And as are spanned athwart a tender cloud
  Two rainbows parallel and like in color,
  When Juno to her handmaid gives command,

(The one without born of the one within,
  Like to the speaking of that vagrant one
  Whom love consumed as doth the sun the vapours,)

And make the people here, through covenant
  God set with Noah, presageful of the world
  That shall no more be covered with a flood,

In such wise of those sempiternal roses
  The garlands twain encompassed us about,
  And thus the outer to the inner answered.

After the dance, and other grand rejoicings,
  Both of the singing, and the flaming forth
  Effulgence with effulgence blithe and tender,

Together, at once, with one accord had stopped,
  (Even as the eyes, that, as volition moves them,
  Must needs together shut and lift themselves,)

Out of the heart of one of the new lights
  There came a voice, that needle to the star
  Made me appear in turning thitherward.

And it began: "The love that makes me fair
  Draws me to speak about the other leader,
  By whom so well is spoken here of mine.

'Tis right, where one is, to bring in the other,
  That, as they were united in their warfare,
  Together likewise may their glory shine.

The soldiery of Christ, which it had cost
  So dear to arm again, behind the standard
  Moved slow and doubtful and in numbers few,

When the Emperor who reigneth evermore
  Provided for the host that was in peril,
  Through grace alone and not that it was worthy;

And, as was said, he to his Bride brought succor
  With champions twain, at whose deed, at whose word
  The straggling people were together drawn.

Within that region where the sweet west wind
  Rises to open the new leaves, wherewith
  Europe is seen to clothe herself afresh,

Not far off from the beating of the waves,
  Behind which in his long career the sun
  Sometimes conceals himself from every man,

Is situate the fortunate Calahorra,
  Under protection of the mighty shield
  In which the Lion subject is and sovereign.

Therein was born the amorous paramour
　Of Christian Faith, the athlete consecrate,
　Kind to his own and cruel to his foes;

And when it was created was his mind
　Replete with such a living energy,
　That in his mother her it made prophetic.

As soon as the espousals were complete
　Between him and the Faith at holy font,
　Where they with mutual safety dowered each other,

The woman, who for him had given assent,
　Saw in a dream the admirable fruit
　That issue would from him and from his heirs;

And that he might be construed as he was,
　A spirit from this place went forth to name him
　With His possessive whose he wholly was.

Dominic was he called; and him I speak of
　Even as of the husbandman whom Christ
　Elected to his garden to assist him.

Envoy and servant sooth he seemed of Christ,
　For the first love made manifest in him
　Was the first counsel that was given by Christ.

Silent and wakeful many a time was he
　Discovered by his nurse upon the ground,
　As if he would have said, 'For this I came.'

O thou his father, Felix verily!
　O thou his mother, verily Joanna,
　If this, interpreted, means as is said!

Not for the world which people toil for now
　In following Ostiense and Taddeo,
　But through his longing after the true manna,

He in short time became so great a teacher,
　That he began to go about the vineyard,
　Which fadeth soon, if faithless be the dresser;

And of the See, (that once was more benignant
 Unto the righteous poor, not through itself,
 But him who sits there and degenerates,)

Not to dispense or two or three for six,
 Not any fortune of first vacancy,
 'Non decimas quae sunt pauperum Dei,'

He asked for, but against the errant world
 Permission to do battle for the seed,
 Of which these four and twenty plants surround thee.

Then with the doctrine and the will together,
 With office apostolical he moved,
 Like torrent which some lofty vein out-presses;

And in among the shoots heretical
 His impetus with greater fury smote,
 Wherever the resistance was the greatest.

Of him were made thereafter divers runnels,
 Whereby the garden catholic is watered,
 So that more living its plantations stand.

If such the one wheel of the Biga was,
 In which the Holy Church itself defended
 And in the field its civic battle won,

Truly full manifest should be to thee
 The excellence of the other, unto whom
 Thomas so courteous was before my coming.

But still the orbit, which the highest part
 Of its circumference made, is derelict,
 So that the mould is where was once the crust.

His family, that had straight forward moved
 With feet upon his footprints, are turned round
 So that they set the point upon the heel.

And soon aware they will be of the harvest
 Of this bad husbandry, when shall the tares
 Complain the granary is taken from them.

Yet say I, he who searcheth leaf by leaf
  Our volume through, would still some page discover
  Where he could read, 'I am as I am wont.'

'Twill not be from Casal nor Acquasparta,
  From whence come such unto the written word
  That one avoids it, and the other narrows.

Bonaventura of Bagnoregio's life
  Am I, who always in great offices
  Postponed considerations sinister.

Here are Illuminato and Agostino,
  Who of the first barefooted beggars were
  That with the cord the friends of God became.

Hugh of Saint Victor is among them here,
  And Peter Mangiador, and Peter of Spain,
  Who down below in volumes twelve is shining;

Nathan the seer, and metropolitan
  Chrysostom, and Anselmus, and Donatus
  Who deigned to lay his hand to the first art;

Here is Rabanus, and beside me here
  Shines the Calabrian Abbot Joachim,
  He with the spirit of prophecy endowed.

To celebrate so great a paladin
  Have moved me the impassioned courtesy
  And the discreet discourses of Friar Thomas,

And with me they have moved this company."

Canto XIII

Let him imagine, who would well conceive
  What now I saw, and let him while I speak
  Retain the image as a steadfast rock,

The fifteen stars, that in their divers regions
  The sky enliven with a light so great
  That it transcends all clusters of the air;

Let him the Wain imagine unto which
  Our vault of heaven sufficeth night and day,
  So that in turning of its pole it fails not;

Let him the mouth imagine of the horn
  That in the point beginneth of the axis
  Round about which the primal wheel revolves,—

To have fashioned of themselves two signs in heaven,
  Like unto that which Minos' daughter made,
  The moment when she felt the frost of death;

And one to have its rays within the other,
  And both to whirl themselves in such a manner
  That one should forward go, the other backward;

And he will have some shadowing forth of that
  True constellation and the double dance
  That circled round the point at which I was;

Because it is as much beyond our wont,
  As swifter than the motion of the Chiana
  Moveth the heaven that all the rest outspeeds.

There sang they neither Bacchus, nor Apollo,
  But in the divine nature Persons three,
  And in one person the divine and human.

The singing and the dance fulfilled their measure,
  And unto us those holy lights gave need,
  Growing in happiness from care to care.

Then broke the silence of those saints concordant
  The light in which the admirable life
  Of God's own mendicant was told to me,

And said: "Now that one straw is trodden out
  Now that its seed is garnered up already,
  Sweet love invites me to thresh out the other.

Into that bosom, thou believest, whence
  Was drawn the rib to form the beauteous cheek
  Whose taste to all the world is costing dear,

And into that which, by the lance transfixed,
  Before and since, such satisfaction made
  That it weighs down the balance of all sin,

Whate'er of light it has to human nature
  Been lawful to possess was all infused
  By the same power that both of them created;

And hence at what I said above dost wonder,
  When I narrated that no second had
  The good which in the fifth light is enclosed.

Now ope thine eyes to what I answer thee,
  And thou shalt see thy creed and my discourse
  Fit in the truth as centre in a circle.

That which can die, and that which dieth not,
  Are nothing but the splendor of the idea
  Which by his love our Lord brings into being;

Because that living Light, which from its fount
  Effulgent flows, so that it disunites not
  From Him nor from the Love in them intrined,

Through its own goodness reunites its rays
  In nine subsistences, as in a mirror,
  Itself eternally remaining One.

Thence it descends to the last potencies,
  Downward from act to act becoming such
  That only brief contingencies it makes;

And these contingencies I hold to be
  Things generated, which the heaven produces
  By its own motion, with seed and without.

Neither their wax, nor that which tempers it,
  Remains immutable, and hence beneath
  The ideal signet more and less shines through;

Therefore it happens, that the selfsame tree
  After its kind bears worse and better fruit,
  And ye are born with characters diverse.

If in perfection tempered were the wax,
  And were the heaven in its supremest virtue,
  The brilliance of the seal would all appear;

But nature gives it evermore deficient,
  In the like manner working as the artist,
  Who has the skill of art and hand that trembles.

If then the fervent Love, the Vision clear,
  Of primal Virtue do dispose and seal,
  Perfection absolute is there acquired.

Thus was of old the earth created worthy
  Of all and every animal perfection;
  And thus the Virgin was impregnate made;

So that thine own opinion I commend,
  That human nature never yet has been,
  Nor will be, what it was in those two persons.

Now if no farther forth I should proceed,
  'Then in what way was he without a peer?'
  Would be the first beginning of thy words.

But, that may well appear what now appears not,
  Think who he was, and what occasion moved him
  To make request, when it was told him, 'Ask.'

I've not so spoken that thou canst not see
  Clearly he was a king who asked for wisdom,
  That he might be sufficiently a king;

'Twas not to know the number in which are
  The motors here above, or if 'necesse'
  With a contingent e'er 'necesse' make,

'Non si est dare primum motum esse,'
  Or if in semicircle can be made
  Triangle so that it have no right angle.

Whence, if thou notest this and what I said,
  A regal prudence is that peerless seeing
  In which the shaft of my intention strikes.

And if on 'rose' thou turnest thy clear eyes,
  Thou'lt see that it has reference alone
  To kings who're many, and the good are rare.

With this distinction take thou what I said,
  And thus it can consist with thy belief
  Of the first father and of our Delight.

And lead shall this be always to thy feet,
  To make thee, like a weary man, move slowly
  Both to the Yes and No thou seest not;

For very low among the fools is he
  Who affirms without distinction, or denies,
  As well in one as in the other case;

Because it happens that full often bends
  Current opinion in the false direction,
  And then the feelings bind the intellect.

Far more than uselessly he leaves the shore,
  (Since he returneth not the same he went,)
  Who fishes for the truth, and has no skill;

And in the world proofs manifest thereof
  Parmenides, Melissus, Brissus are,
  And many who went on and knew not whither;

Thus did Sabellius, Arius, and those fools
  Who have been even as swords unto the Scriptures
  In rendering distorted their straight faces.

Nor yet shall people be too confident
  In judging, even as he is who doth count
  The corn in field or ever it be ripe.

For I have seen all winter long the thorn
  First show itself intractable and fierce,
  And after bear the rose upon its top;

And I have seen a ship direct and swift
  Run o'er the sea throughout its course entire,
  To perish at the harbour's mouth at last.

Let not Dame Bertha nor Ser Martin think,
  Seeing one steal, another offering make,
  To see them in the arbitrament divine;

For one may rise, and fall the other may."

Canto XIV

From centre unto rim, from rim to centre,
  In a round vase the water moves itself,
  As from without 'tis struck or from within.

Into my mind upon a sudden dropped
  What I am saying, at the moment when
  Silent became the glorious life of Thomas,

Because of the resemblance that was born
  Of his discourse and that of Beatrice,
  Whom, after him, it pleased thus to begin:

"This man has need (and does not tell you so,
  Nor with the voice, nor even in his thought)
  Of going to the root of one truth more.

Declare unto him if the light wherewith
  Blossoms your substance shall remain with you
  Eternally the same that it is now;

And if it do remain, say in what manner,
  After ye are again made visible,
  It can be that it injure not your sight."

As by a greater gladness urged and drawn
  They who are dancing in a ring sometimes
  Uplift their voices and their motions quicken;

So, at that orison devout and prompt,
  The holy circles a new joy displayed
  In their revolving and their wondrous song.

Whoso lamenteth him that here we die
  That we may live above, has never there
  Seen the refreshment of the eternal rain.

The One and Two and Three who ever liveth,
  And reigneth ever in Three and Two and One,
  Not circumscribed and all things circumscribing,

Three several times was chanted by each one
  Among those spirits, with such melody
  That for all merit it were just reward;

And, in the lustre most divine of all
  The lesser ring, I heard a modest voice,
  Such as perhaps the Angel's was to Mary,

Answer: "As long as the festivity
  Of Paradise shall be, so long our love
  Shall radiate round about us such a vesture.

Its brightness is proportioned to the ardour,
  The ardour to the vision; and the vision
  Equals what grace it has above its worth.

When, glorious and sanctified, our flesh
  Is reassumed, then shall our persons be
  More pleasing by their being all complete;

For will increase whate'er bestows on us
  Of light gratuitous the Good Supreme,
  Light which enables us to look on Him;

Therefore the vision must perforce increase,
  Increase the ardour which from that is kindled,
  Increase the radiance which from this proceeds.

But even as a coal that sends forth flame,
  And by its vivid whiteness overpowers it
  So that its own appearance it maintains,

Thus the effulgence that surrounds us now
  Shall be o'erpowered in aspect by the flesh,
  Which still to-day the earth doth cover up;

Nor can so great a splendor weary us,
  For strong will be the organs of the body
  To everything which hath the power to please us."

So sudden and alert appeared to me
  Both one and the other choir to say Amen,
  That well they showed desire for their dead bodies;

Nor sole for them perhaps, but for the mothers,
  The fathers, and the rest who had been dear
  Or ever they became eternal flames.

And lo! all round about of equal brightness
  Arose a lustre over what was there,
  Like an horizon that is clearing up.

And as at rise of early eve begin
  Along the welkin new appearances,
  So that the sight seems real and unreal,

It seemed to me that new subsistences
  Began there to be seen, and make a circle
  Outside the other two circumferences.

O very sparkling of the Holy Spirit,
  How sudden and incandescent it became
  Unto mine eyes, that vanquished bore it not!

But Beatrice so beautiful and smiling
  Appeared to me, that with the other sights
  That followed not my memory I must leave her.

Then to uplift themselves mine eyes resumed
  The power, and I beheld myself translated
  To higher salvation with my Lady only.

Well was I ware that I was more uplifted
  By the enkindled smiling of the star,
  That seemed to me more ruddy than its wont.

With all my heart, and in that dialect
  Which is the same in all, such holocaust
  To God I made as the new grace beseemed;

And not yet from my bosom was exhausted
  The ardour of sacrifice, before I knew
  This offering was accepted and auspicious;

For with so great a lustre and so red
  Splendors appeared to me in twofold rays,
  I said: "O Helios who dost so adorn them!"

Even as distinct with less and greater lights
  Glimmers between the two poles of the world
  The Galaxy that maketh wise men doubt,

Thus constellated in the depths of Mars,
  Those rays described the venerable sign
  That quadrants joining in a circle make.

Here doth my memory overcome my genius;
  For on that cross as levin gleamed forth Christ,
  So that I cannot find ensample worthy;

But he who takes his cross and follows Christ
  Again will pardon me what I omit,
  Seeing in that aurora lighten Christ.

From horn to horn, and 'twixt the top and base,
  Lights were in motion, brightly scintillating
  As they together met and passed each other;

Thus level and aslant and swift and slow
  We here behold, renewing still the sight,
  The particles of bodies long and short,

Across the sunbeam move, wherewith is listed
  Sometimes the shade, which for their own defence
  People with cunning and with art contrive.

And as a lute and harp, accordant strung
  With many strings, a dulcet tinkling make
  To him by whom the notes are not distinguished,

So from the lights that there to me appeared
  Upgathered through the cross a melody,
  Which rapt me, not distinguishing the hymn.

Well was I ware it was of lofty laud,
  Because there came to me, "Arise and conquer!"
  As unto him who hears and comprehends not.

So much enamoured I became therewith,
  That until then there was not anything
  That e'er had fettered me with such sweet bonds.

Perhaps my word appears somewhat too bold,
  Postponing the delight of those fair eyes,
  Into which gazing my desire has rest;

But who bethinks him that the living seals
  Of every beauty grow in power ascending,
  And that I there had not turned round to those,

Can me excuse, if I myself accuse
  To excuse myself, and see that I speak truly:
  For here the holy joy is not disclosed,

Because ascending it becomes more pure.

Canto XV

A will benign, in which reveals itself
  Ever the love that righteously inspires,
  As in the iniquitous, cupidity,

Silence imposed upon that dulcet lyre,
  And quieted the consecrated chords,
  That Heaven's right hand doth tighten and relax.

How unto just entreaties shall be deaf
  Those substances, which, to give me desire
  Of praying them, with one accord grew silent?

'Tis well that without end he should lament,
  Who for the love of thing that doth not last
  Eternally despoils him of that love!

As through the pure and tranquil evening air
  There shoots from time to time a sudden fire,
  Moving the eyes that steadfast were before,

And seems to be a star that changeth place,
  Except that in the part where it is kindled
  Nothing is missed, and this endureth little;

So from the horn that to the right extends
  Unto that cross's foot there ran a star
  Out of the constellation shining there;

Nor was the gem dissevered from its ribbon,
  But down the radiant fillet ran along,
  So that fire seemed it behind alabaster.

Thus piteous did Anchises' shade reach forward,
  If any faith our greatest Muse deserve,
  When in Elysium he his son perceived.

"O sanguis meus, O superinfusa
  Gratia Dei, sicut tibi, cui
  Bis unquam Coeli janua reclusa?"

Thus that effulgence; whence I gave it heed;
  Then round unto my Lady turned my sight,
  And on this side and that was stupefied;

For in her eyes was burning such a smile
  That with mine own methought I touched the bottom
  Both of my grace and of my Paradise!

Then, pleasant to the hearing and the sight,
  The spirit joined to its beginning things
  I understood not, so profound it spake;

Nor did it hide itself from me by choice,
  But by necessity; for its conception
  Above the mark of mortals set itself.

And when the bow of burning sympathy
  Was so far slackened, that its speech descended
  Towards the mark of our intelligence,

The first thing that was understood by me
  Was "Benedight be Thou, O Trine and One,
  Who hast unto my seed so courteous been!"

And it continued: "Hunger long and grateful,
  Drawn from the reading of the mighty volume
  Wherein is never changed the white nor dark,

Thou hast appeased, my son, within this light
  In which I speak to thee, by grace of her
  Who to this lofty flight with plumage clothed thee.

Thou thinkest that to me thy thought doth pass
  From Him who is the first, as from the unit,
  If that be known, ray out the five and six;

And therefore who I am thou askest not,
  And why I seem more joyous unto thee
  Than any other of this gladsome crowd.

Thou think'st the truth; because the small and great
  Of this existence look into the mirror
  Wherein, before thou think'st, thy thought thou showest.

But that the sacred love, in which I watch
  With sight perpetual, and which makes me thirst
  With sweet desire, may better be fulfilled,

Now let thy voice secure and frank and glad
  Proclaim the wishes, the desire proclaim,
  To which my answer is decreed already."

To Beatrice I turned me, and she heard
  Before I spake, and smiled to me a sign,
  That made the wings of my desire increase;

Then in this wise began I: "Love and knowledge,
  When on you dawned the first Equality,
  Of the same weight for each of you became;

For in the Sun, which lighted you and burned
  With heat and radiance, they so equal are,
  That all similitudes are insufficient.

But among mortals will and argument,
  For reason that to you is manifest,
  Diversely feathered in their pinions are.

Whence I, who mortal am, feel in myself
  This inequality; so give not thanks,
  Save in my heart, for this paternal welcome.

Truly do I entreat thee, living topaz!
  Set in this precious jewel as a gem,
  That thou wilt satisfy me with thy name."

"O leaf of mine, in whom I pleasure took
  E'en while awaiting, I was thine own root!"
  Such a beginning he in answer made me.

Then said to me: "That one from whom is named
  Thy race, and who a hundred years and more
  Has circled round the mount on the first cornice,

A son of mine and thy great-grandsire was;
  Well it behoves thee that the long fatigue
  Thou shouldst for him make shorter with thy works.

Florence, within the ancient boundary
  From which she taketh still her tierce and nones,
  Abode in quiet, temperate and chaste.

No golden chain she had, nor coronal,
  Nor ladies shod with sandal shoon, nor girdle
  That caught the eye more than the person did.

Not yet the daughter at her birth struck fear
  Into the father, for the time and dower
  Did not o'errun this side or that the measure.

No houses had she void of families,
  Not yet had thither come Sardanapalus
  To show what in a chamber can be done;

Not yet surpassed had Montemalo been
  By your Uccellatojo, which surpassed
  Shall in its downfall be as in its rise.

Bellincion Berti saw I go begirt
  With leather and with bone, and from the mirror
  His dame depart without a painted face;

And him of Nerli saw, and him of Vecchio,
  Contented with their simple suits of buff
  And with the spindle and the flax their dames.

O fortunate women! and each one was certain
  Of her own burial-place, and none as yet
  For sake of France was in her bed deserted.

One o'er the cradle kept her studious watch,
  And in her lullaby the language used
  That first delights the fathers and the mothers;

Another, drawing tresses from her distaff,
  Told o'er among her family the tales
  Of Trojans and of Fesole and Rome.

As great a marvel then would have been held
  A Lapo Salterello, a Cianghella,
  As Cincinnatus or Cornelia now.

To such a quiet, such a beautiful
  Life of the citizen, to such a safe
  Community, and to so sweet an inn,

Did Mary give me, with loud cries invoked,
  And in your ancient Baptistery at once
  Christian and Cacciaguida I became.

Moronto was my brother, and Eliseo;
  From Val di Pado came to me my wife,
  And from that place thy surname was derived.

I followed afterward the Emperor Conrad,
  And he begirt me of his chivalry,
  So much I pleased him with my noble deeds.

I followed in his train against that law's
  Iniquity, whose people doth usurp
  Your just possession, through your Pastor's fault.

There by that execrable race was I
  Released from bonds of the fallacious world,
  The love of which defileth many souls,

And came from martyrdom unto this peace."

Canto XVI

O thou our poor nobility of blood,
  If thou dost make the people glory in thee
  Down here where our affection languishes,

A marvellous thing it ne'er will be to me;
  For there where appetite is not perverted,
  I say in Heaven, of thee I made a boast!

Truly thou art a cloak that quickly shortens,
  So that unless we piece thee day by day
  Time goeth round about thee with his shears!

With 'You,' which Rome was first to tolerate,
  (Wherein her family less perseveres,)
  Yet once again my words beginning made;

Whence Beatrice, who stood somewhat apart,
  Smiling, appeared like unto her who coughed
  At the first failing writ of Guenever.

And I began: "You are my ancestor,
  You give to me all hardihood to speak,
  You lift me so that I am more than I.

So many rivulets with gladness fill
  My mind, that of itself it makes a joy
  Because it can endure this and not burst.

Then tell me, my beloved root ancestral,
  Who were your ancestors, and what the years
  That in your boyhood chronicled themselves?

Tell me about the sheepfold of Saint John,
  How large it was, and who the people were
  Within it worthy of the highest seats."

As at the blowing of the winds a coal
  Quickens to flame, so I beheld that light
  Become resplendent at my blandishments.

And as unto mine eyes it grew more fair,
  With voice more sweet and tender, but not in
  This modern dialect, it said to me:

"From uttering of the 'Ave,' till the birth
  In which my mother, who is now a saint,
  Of me was lightened who had been her burden,

Unto its Lion had this fire returned
  Five hundred fifty times and thirty more,
  To reinflame itself beneath his paw.

My ancestors and I our birthplace had
  Where first is found the last ward of the city
  By him who runneth in your annual game.

Suffice it of my elders to hear this;
  But who they were, and whence they thither came,
  Silence is more considerate than speech.

All those who at that time were there between
  Mars and the Baptist, fit for bearing arms,
  Were a fifth part of those who now are living;

But the community, that now is mixed
  With Campi and Certaldo and Figghine,
  Pure in the lowest artisan was seen.

O how much better 'twere to have as neighbors
  The folk of whom I speak, and at Galluzzo
  And at Trespiano have your boundary,

Than have them in the town, and bear the stench
  Of Aguglione's churl, and him of Signa
  Who has sharp eyes for trickery already.

Had not the folk, which most of all the world
  Degenerates, been a step-dame unto Caesar,
  But as a mother to her son benignant,

Some who turn Florentines, and trade and discount,
  Would have gone back again to Simifonte
  There where their grandsires went about as beggars.

At Montemurlo still would be the Counts,
  The Cerchi in the parish of Acone,
  Perhaps in Valdigrieve the Buondelmonti.

Ever the intermingling of the people
  Has been the source of malady in cities,
  As in the body food it surfeits on;

And a blind bull more headlong plunges down
  Than a blind lamb; and very often cuts
  Better and more a single sword than five.

If Luni thou regard, and Urbisaglia,
  How they have passed away, and how are passing
  Chiusi and Sinigaglia after them,

To hear how races waste themselves away,
  Will seem to thee no novel thing nor hard,
  Seeing that even cities have an end.

All things of yours have their mortality,
  Even as yourselves; but it is hidden in some
  That a long while endure, and lives are short;

And as the turning of the lunar heaven
  Covers and bares the shores without a pause,
  In the like manner fortune does with Florence.

Therefore should not appear a marvellous thing
  What I shall say of the great Florentines
  Of whom the fame is hidden in the Past.

I saw the Ughi, saw the Catellini,
  Filippi, Greci, Ormanni, and Alberichi,
  Even in their fall illustrious citizens;

And saw, as mighty as they ancient were,
  With him of La Sannella him of Arca,
  And Soldanier, Ardinghi, and Bostichi.

Near to the gate that is at present laden
  With a new felony of so much weight
  That soon it shall be jetsam from the bark,

The Ravignani were, from whom descended
  The County Guido, and whoe'er the name
  Of the great Bellincione since hath taken.

He of La Pressa knew the art of ruling
  Already, and already Galigajo
  Had hilt and pommel gilded in his house.

Mighty already was the Column Vair,
  Sacchetti, Giuochi, Fifant, and Barucci,
  And Galli, and they who for the bushel blush.

The stock from which were the Calfucci born
  Was great already, and already chosen
  To curule chairs the Sizii and Arrigucci.

O how beheld I those who are undone
  By their own pride! and how the Balls of Gold
  Florence enflowered in all their mighty deeds!

So likewise did the ancestors of those
  Who evermore, when vacant is your church,
  Fatten by staying in consistory.

The insolent race, that like a dragon follows
  Whoever flees, and unto him that shows
  His teeth or purse is gentle as a lamb,

Already rising was, but from low people;
  So that it pleased not Ubertin Donato
  That his wife's father should make him their kin.

Already had Caponsacco to the Market
  From Fesole descended, and already
  Giuda and Infangato were good burghers.

I'll tell a thing incredible, but true;
  One entered the small circuit by a gate
  Which from the Della Pera took its name!

Each one that bears the beautiful escutcheon
  Of the great baron whose renown and name
  The festival of Thomas keepeth fresh,

Knighthood and privilege from him received;
  Though with the populace unites himself
  To-day the man who binds it with a border.

Already were Gualterotti and Importuni;
  And still more quiet would the Borgo be
  If with new neighbors it remained unfed.

The house from which is born your lamentation,
  Through just disdain that death among you brought
  And put an end unto your joyous life,

Was honored in itself and its companions.
  O Buondelmonte, how in evil hour
  Thou fled'st the bridal at another's promptings!

Many would be rejoicing who are sad,
  If God had thee surrendered to the Ema
  The first time that thou camest to the city.

But it behoved the mutilated stone
  Which guards the bridge, that Florence should provide
  A victim in her latest hour of peace.

With all these families, and others with them,
  Florence beheld I in so great repose,
  That no occasion had she whence to weep;

With all these families beheld so just
  And glorious her people, that the lily
  Never upon the spear was placed reversed,

Nor by division was vermilion made."

Canto XVII

As came to Clymene, to be made certain
  Of that which he had heard against himself,
  He who makes fathers chary still to children,

Even such was I, and such was I perceived
  By Beatrice and by the holy light
  That first on my account had changed its place.

Therefore my Lady said to me: "Send forth
 The flame of thy desire, so that it issue
 Imprinted well with the internal stamp;

Not that our knowledge may be greater made
 By speech of thine, but to accustom thee
 To tell thy thirst, that we may give thee drink."

"O my beloved tree, (that so dost lift thee,
 That even as minds terrestrial perceive
 No triangle containeth two obtuse,

So thou beholdest the contingent things
 Ere in themselves they are, fixing thine eyes
 Upon the point in which all times are present,)

While I was with Virgilius conjoined
 Upon the mountain that the souls doth heal,
 And when descending into the dead world,

Were spoken to me of my future life
 Some grievous words; although I feel myself
 In sooth foursquare against the blows of chance.

On this account my wish would be content
 To hear what fortune is approaching me,
 Because foreseen an arrow comes more slowly."

Thus did I say unto that selfsame light
 That unto me had spoken before; and even
 As Beatrice willed was my own will confessed.

Not in vague phrase, in which the foolish folk
 Ensnared themselves of old, ere yet was slain
 The Lamb of God who taketh sins away,

But with clear words and unambiguous
 Language responded that paternal love,
 Hid and revealed by its own proper smile:

"Contingency, that outside of the volume
 Of your materiality extends not,
 Is all depicted in the eternal aspect.

Necessity however thence it takes not,
  Except as from the eye, in which 'tis mirrored,
  A ship that with the current down descends.

From thence, e'en as there cometh to the ear
  Sweet harmony from an organ, comes in sight
  To me the time that is preparing for thee.

As forth from Athens went Hippolytus,
  By reason of his step-dame false and cruel,
  So thou from Florence must perforce depart.

Already this is willed, and this is sought for;
  And soon it shall be done by him who thinks it,
  Where every day the Christ is bought and sold.

The blame shall follow the offended party
  In outcry as is usual; but the vengeance
  Shall witness to the truth that doth dispense it.

Thou shalt abandon everything beloved
  Most tenderly, and this the arrow is
  Which first the bow of banishment shoots forth.

Thou shalt have proof how savoureth of salt
  The bread of others, and how hard a road
  The going down and up another's stairs.

And that which most shall weigh upon thy shoulders
  Will be the bad and foolish company
  With which into this valley thou shalt fall;

For all ingrate, all mad and impious
  Will they become against thee; but soon after
  They, and not thou, shall have the forehead scarlet.

Of their bestiality their own proceedings
  Shall furnish proof; so 'twill be well for thee
  A party to have made thee by thyself.

Thine earliest refuge and thine earliest inn
  Shall be the mighty Lombard's courtesy,
  Who on the Ladder bears the holy bird,

Who such benign regard shall have for thee
  That 'twixt you twain, in doing and in asking,
  That shall be first which is with others last.

With him shalt thou see one who at his birth
  Has by this star of strength been so impressed,
  That notable shall his achievements be.

Not yet the people are aware of him
  Through his young age, since only nine years yet
  Around about him have these wheels revolved.

But ere the Gascon cheat the noble Henry,
  Some sparkles of his virtue shall appear
  In caring not for silver nor for toil.

So recognized shall his magnificence
  Become hereafter, that his enemies
  Will not have power to keep mute tongues about it.

On him rely, and on his benefits;
  By him shall many people be transformed,
  Changing condition rich and mendicant;

And written in thy mind thou hence shalt bear
  Of him, but shalt not say it"—and things said he
  Incredible to those who shall be present.

Then added: "Son, these are the commentaries
  On what was said to thee; behold the snares
  That are concealed behind few revolutions;

Yet would I not thy neighbors thou shouldst envy,
  Because thy life into the future reaches
  Beyond the punishment of their perfidies."

When by its silence showed that sainted soul
  That it had finished putting in the woof
  Into that web which I had given it warped,

Began I, even as he who yearneth after,
  Being in doubt, some counsel from a person
  Who seeth, and uprightly wills, and loves:

"Well see I, father mine, how spurreth on
   The time towards me such a blow to deal me
   As heaviest is to him who most gives way.

Therefore with foresight it is well I arm me,
   That, if the dearest place be taken from me,
   I may not lose the others by my songs.

Down through the world of infinite bitterness,
   And o'er the mountain, from whose beauteous summit
   The eyes of my own Lady lifted me,

And afterward through heaven from light to light,
   I have learned that which, if I tell again,
   Will be a savour of strong herbs to many.

And if I am a timid friend to truth,
   I fear lest I may lose my life with those
   Who will hereafter call this time the olden."

The light in which was smiling my own treasure
   Which there I had discovered, flashed at first
   As in the sunshine doth a golden mirror;

Then made reply: "A conscience overcast
   Or with its own or with another's shame,
   Will taste forsooth the tartness of thy word;

But ne'ertheless, all falsehood laid aside,
   Make manifest thy vision utterly,
   And let them scratch wherever is the itch;

For if thine utterance shall offensive be
   At the first taste, a vital nutriment
   'Twill leave thereafter, when it is digested.

This cry of thine shall do as doth the wind,
   Which smiteth most the most exalted summits,
   And that is no slight argument of honor.

Therefore are shown to thee within these wheels,
   Upon the mount and in the dolorous valley,
   Only the souls that unto fame are known;

Because the spirit of the hearer rests not,
  Nor doth confirm its faith by an example
  Which has the root of it unknown and hidden,

Or other reason that is not apparent."

Canto XVIII

Now was alone rejoicing in its word
  That soul beatified, and I was tasting
  My own, the bitter tempering with the sweet,

And the Lady who to God was leading me
  Said: "Change thy thought; consider that I am
  Near unto Him who every wrong disburdens."

Unto the loving accents of my comfort
  I turned me round, and then what love I saw
  Within those holy eyes I here relinquish;

Not only that my language I distrust,
  But that my mind cannot return so far
  Above itself, unless another guide it.

Thus much upon that point can I repeat,
  That, her again beholding, my affection
  From every other longing was released.

While the eternal pleasure, which direct
  Rayed upon Beatrice, from her fair face
  Contented me with its reflected aspect,

Conquering me with the radiance of a smile,
  She said to me, "Turn thee about and listen;
  Not in mine eyes alone is Paradise."

Even as sometimes here do we behold
  The affection in the look, if it be such
  That all the soul is wrapt away by it,

So, by the flaming of the effulgence holy
  To which I turned, I recognized therein
  The wish of speaking to me somewhat farther.

And it began: "In this fifth resting-place
  Upon the tree that liveth by its summit,
  And aye bears fruit, and never loses leaf,

Are blessed spirits that below, ere yet
  They came to Heaven, were of such great renown
  That every Muse therewith would affluent be.

Therefore look thou upon the cross's horns;
  He whom I now shall name will there enact
  What doth within a cloud its own swift fire."

I saw athwart the Cross a splendor drawn
  By naming Joshua, (even as he did it,)
  Nor noted I the word before the deed;

And at the name of the great Maccabee
  I saw another move itself revolving,
  And gladness was the whip unto that top.

Likewise for Charlemagne and for Orlando,
  Two of them my regard attentive followed
  As followeth the eye its falcon flying.

William thereafterward, and Renouard,
  And the Duke Godfrey, did attract my sight
  Along upon that Cross, and Robert Guiscard.

Then, moved and mingled with the other lights,
  The soul that had addressed me showed how great
  An artist 'twas among the heavenly singers.

To my right side I turned myself around,
  My duty to behold in Beatrice
  Either by words or gesture signified;

And so translucent I beheld her eyes,
  So full of pleasure, that her countenance
  Surpassed its other and its latest wont.

And as, by feeling greater delectation,
  A man in doing good from day to day
  Becomes aware his virtue is increasing,

So I became aware that my gyration
  With heaven together had increased its arc,
  That miracle beholding more adorned.

And such as is the change, in little lapse
  Of time, in a pale woman, when her face
  Is from the load of bashfulness unladen,

Such was it in mine eyes, when I had turned,
  Caused by the whiteness of the temperate star,
  The sixth, which to itself had gathered me.

Within that Jovial torch did I behold
  The sparkling of the love which was therein
  Delineate our language to mine eyes.

And even as birds uprisen from the shore,
  As in congratulation o'er their food,
  Make squadrons of themselves, now round, now long,

So from within those lights the holy creatures
  Sang flying to and fro, and in their figures
  Made of themselves now D, now I, now L.

First singing they to their own music moved;
  Then one becoming of these characters,
  A little while they rested and were silent.

O divine Pegasea, thou who genius
  Dost glorious make, and render it long-lived,
  And this through thee the cities and the kingdoms,

Illume me with thyself, that I may bring
  Their figures out as I have them conceived!
  Apparent be thy power in these brief verses!

Themselves then they displayed in five times seven
  Vowels and consonants; and I observed
  The parts as they seemed spoken unto me.

'Diligite justitiam,' these were
  First verb and noun of all that was depicted;
  'Qui judicatis terram' were the last.

Thereafter in the M of the fifth word
  Remained they so arranged, that Jupiter
  Seemed to be silver there with gold inlaid.

And other lights I saw descend where was
  The summit of the M, and pause there singing
  The good, I think, that draws them to itself.

Then, as in striking upon burning logs
  Upward there fly innumerable sparks,
  Whence fools are wont to look for auguries,

More than a thousand lights seemed thence to rise,
  And to ascend, some more, and others less,
  Even as the Sun that lights them had allotted;

And, each one being quiet in its place,
  The head and neck beheld I of an eagle
  Delineated by that inlaid fire.

He who there paints has none to be his guide;
  But Himself guides; and is from Him remembered
  That virtue which is form unto the nest.

The other beatitude, that contented seemed
  At first to bloom a lily on the M,
  By a slight motion followed out the imprint.

O gentle star! what and how many gems
  Did demonstrate to me, that all our justice
  Effect is of that heaven which thou ingemmest!

Wherefore I pray the Mind, in which begin
  Thy motion and thy virtue, to regard
  Whence comes the smoke that vitiates thy rays;

So that a second time it now be wroth
  With buying and with selling in the temple
  Whose walls were built with signs and martyrdoms!

O soldiery of heaven, whom I contemplate,
  Implore for those who are upon the earth
  All gone astray after the bad example!

Once 'twas the custom to make war with swords;
  But now 'tis made by taking here and there
  The bread the pitying Father shuts from none.

Yet thou, who writest but to cancel, think
  That Peter and that Paul, who for this vineyard
  Which thou art spoiling died, are still alive!

Well canst thou say: "So steadfast my desire
  Is unto him who willed to live alone,
  And for a dance was led to martyrdom,

That I know not the Fisherman nor Paul."

Canto XIX

Appeared before me with its wings outspread
  The beautiful image that in sweet fruition
  Made jubilant the interwoven souls;

Appeared a little ruby each, wherein
  Ray of the sun was burning so enkindled
  That each into mine eyes refracted it.

And what it now behoves me to retrace
  Nor voice has e'er reported, nor ink written,
  Nor was by fantasy e'er comprehended;

For speak I saw, and likewise heard, the beak,
  And utter with its voice both 'I' and 'My,'
  When in conception it was 'We' and 'Our.'

And it began: "Being just and merciful
  Am I exalted here unto that glory
  Which cannot be exceeded by desire;

And upon earth I left my memory
  Such, that the evil-minded people there
  Commend it, but continue not the story."

So doth a single heat from many embers
  Make itself felt, even as from many loves
  Issued a single sound from out that image.

Whence I thereafter: "O perpetual flowers
  Of the eternal joy, that only one
  Make me perceive your odours manifold,

Exhaling, break within me the great fast
  Which a long season has in hunger held me,
  Not finding for it any food on earth.

Well do I know, that if in heaven its mirror
  Justice Divine another realm doth make,
  Yours apprehends it not through any veil.

You know how I attentively address me
  To listen; and you know what is the doubt
  That is in me so very old a fast."

Even as a falcon, issuing from his hood,
  Doth move his head, and with his wings applaud him,
  Showing desire, and making himself fine,

Saw I become that standard, which of lauds
  Was interwoven of the grace divine,
  With such songs as he knows who there rejoices.

Then it began: "He who a compass turned
  On the world's outer verge, and who within it
  Devised so much occult and manifest,

Could not the impress of his power so make
  On all the universe, as that his Word
  Should not remain in infinite excess.

And this makes certain that the first proud being,
  Who was the paragon of every creature,
  By not awaiting light fell immature.

And hence appears it, that each minor nature
  Is scant receptacle unto that good
  Which has no end, and by itself is measured.

In consequence our vision, which perforce
  Must be some ray of that intelligence
  With which all things whatever are replete,

Cannot in its own nature be so potent,
  That it shall not its origin discern
  Far beyond that which is apparent to it.

Therefore into the justice sempiternal
  The power of vision that your world receives,
  As eye into the ocean, penetrates;

Which, though it see the bottom near the shore,
  Upon the deep perceives it not, and yet
  'Tis there, but it is hidden by the depth.

There is no light but comes from the serene
  That never is o'ercast, nay, it is darkness
  Or shadow of the flesh, or else its poison.

Amply to thee is opened now the cavern
  Which has concealed from thee the living justice
  Of which thou mad'st such frequent questioning.

For saidst thou: 'Born a man is on the shore
  Of Indus, and is none who there can speak
  Of Christ, nor who can read, nor who can write;

And all his inclinations and his actions
  Are good, so far as human reason sees,
  Without a sin in life or in discourse:

He dieth unbaptised and without faith;
  Where is this justice that condemneth him?
  Where is his fault, if he do not believe?'

Now who art thou, that on the bench wouldst sit
  In judgment at a thousand miles away,
  With the short vision of a single span?

Truly to him who with me subtilizes,
  If so the Scripture were not over you,
  For doubting there were marvellous occasion.

O animals terrene, O stolid minds,
  The primal will, that in itself is good,
  Ne'er from itself, the Good Supreme, has moved.

So much is just as is accordant with it;
  No good created draws it to itself,
  But it, by raying forth, occasions that."

Even as above her nest goes circling round
  The stork when she has fed her little ones,
  And he who has been fed looks up at her,

So lifted I my brows, and even such
  Became the blessed image, which its wings
  Was moving, by so many counsels urged.

Circling around it sang, and said: "As are
  My notes to thee, who dost not comprehend them,
  Such is the eternal judgment to you mortals."

Those lucent splendors of the Holy Spirit
  Grew quiet then, but still within the standard
  That made the Romans reverend to the world.

It recommenced: "Unto this kingdom never
  Ascended one who had not faith in Christ,
  Before or since he to the tree was nailed.

But look thou, many crying are, 'Christ, Christ!'
  Who at the judgment shall be far less near
  To him than some shall be who knew not Christ.

Such Christians shall the Ethiop condemn,
  When the two companies shall be divided,
  The one for ever rich, the other poor.

What to your kings may not the Persians say,
  When they that volume opened shall behold
  In which are written down all their dispraises?

There shall be seen, among the deeds of Albert,
  That which ere long shall set the pen in motion,
  For which the realm of Prague shall be deserted.

There shall be seen the woe that on the Seine
  He brings by falsifying of the coin,
  Who by the blow of a wild boar shall die.

There shall be seen the pride that causes thirst,
  Which makes the Scot and Englishman so mad
  That they within their boundaries cannot rest;

Be seen the luxury and effeminate life
  Of him of Spain, and the Bohemian,
  Who valour never knew and never wished;

Be seen the Cripple of Jerusalem,
  His goodness represented by an I,
  While the reverse an M shall represent;

Be seen the avarice and poltroonery
  Of him who guards the Island of the Fire,
  Wherein Anchises finished his long life;

And to declare how pitiful he is
  Shall be his record in contracted letters
  Which shall make note of much in little space.

And shall appear to each one the foul deeds
  Of uncle and of brother who a nation
  So famous have dishonored, and two crowns.

And he of Portugal and he of Norway
  Shall there be known, and he of Rascia too,
  Who saw in evil hour the coin of Venice.

O happy Hungary, if she let herself
  Be wronged no farther! and Navarre the happy,
  If with the hills that gird her she be armed!

And each one may believe that now, as hansel
  Thereof, do Nicosia and Famagosta
  Lament and rage because of their own beast,

Who from the others' flank departeth not."

Canto XX

When he who all the world illuminates
  Out of our hemisphere so far descends
  That on all sides the daylight is consumed,

The heaven, that erst by him alone was kindled,
  Doth suddenly reveal itself again
  By many lights, wherein is one resplendent.

And came into my mind this act of heaven,
  When the ensign of the world and of its leaders
  Had silent in the blessed beak become;

Because those living luminaries all,
  By far more luminous, did songs begin
  Lapsing and falling from my memory.

O gentle Love, that with a smile dost cloak thee,
  How ardent in those sparks didst thou appear,
  That had the breath alone of holy thoughts!

After the precious and pellucid crystals,
  With which begemmed the sixth light I beheld,
  Silence imposed on the angelic bells,

I seemed to hear the murmuring of a river
  That clear descendeth down from rock to rock,
  Showing the affluence of its mountain-top.

And as the sound upon the cithern's neck
  Taketh its form, and as upon the vent
  Of rustic pipe the wind that enters it,

Even thus, relieved from the delay of waiting,
  That murmuring of the eagle mounted up
  Along its neck, as if it had been hollow.

There it became a voice, and issued thence
  From out its beak, in such a form of words
  As the heart waited for wherein I wrote them.

"The part in me which sees and bears the sun
  In mortal eagles," it began to me,
  "Now fixedly must needs be looked upon;

For of the fires of which I make my figure,
  Those whence the eye doth sparkle in my head
  Of all their orders the supremest are.

He who is shining in the midst as pupil
  Was once the singer of the Holy Spirit,
  Who bore the ark from city unto city;

Now knoweth he the merit of his song,
  In so far as effect of his own counsel,
  By the reward which is commensurate.

Of five, that make a circle for my brow,
  He that approacheth nearest to my beak
  Did the poor widow for her son console;

Now knoweth he how dearly it doth cost
  Not following Christ, by the experience
  Of this sweet life and of its opposite.

He who comes next in the circumference
  Of which I speak, upon its highest arc,
  Did death postpone by penitence sincere;

Now knoweth he that the eternal judgment
  Suffers no change, albeit worthy prayer
  Maketh below to-morrow of to-day.

The next who follows, with the laws and me,
  Under the good intent that bore bad fruit
  Became a Greek by ceding to the pastor;

Now knoweth he how all the ill deduced
  From his good action is not harmful to him,
  Although the world thereby may be destroyed.

And he, whom in the downward arc thou seest,
  Guglielmo was, whom the same land deplores
  That weepeth Charles and Frederick yet alive;

Now knoweth he how heaven enamoured is
  With a just king; and in the outward show
  Of his effulgence he reveals it still.

Who would believe, down in the errant world,
  That e'er the Trojan Ripheus in this round
  Could be the fifth one of the holy lights?

Now knoweth he enough of what the world
  Has not the power to see of grace divine,
  Although his sight may not discern the bottom."

Like as a lark that in the air expatiates,
  First singing and then silent with content
  Of the last sweetness that doth satisfy her,

Such seemed to me the image of the imprint
  Of the eternal pleasure, by whose will
  Doth everything become the thing it is.

And notwithstanding to my doubt I was
  As glass is to the color that invests it,
  To wait the time in silence it endured not,

But forth from out my mouth, "What things are these?"
  Extorted with the force of its own weight;
  Whereat I saw great joy of coruscation.

Thereafterward with eye still more enkindled
  The blessed standard made to me reply,
  To keep me not in wonderment suspended:

"I see that thou believest in these things
  Because I say them, but thou seest not how;
  So that, although believed in, they are hidden.

Thou doest as he doth who a thing by name
  Well apprehendeth, but its quiddity
  Cannot perceive, unless another show it.

'Regnum coelorum' suffereth violence
  From fervent love, and from that living hope
  That overcometh the Divine volition;

Not in the guise that man o'ercometh man,
  But conquers it because it will be conquered,
  And conquered conquers by benignity.

The first life of the eyebrow and the fifth
  Cause thee astonishment, because with them
  Thou seest the region of the angels painted.

They passed not from their bodies, as thou thinkest,
  Gentiles, but Christians in the steadfast faith
  Of feet that were to suffer and had suffered.

For one from Hell, where no one e'er turns back
  Unto good will, returned unto his bones,
  And that of living hope was the reward,—

Of living hope, that placed its efficacy
  In prayers to God made to resuscitate him,
  So that 'twere possible to move his will.

The glorious soul concerning which I speak,
  Returning to the flesh, where brief its stay,
  Believed in Him who had the power to aid it;

And, in believing, kindled to such fire
  Of genuine love, that at the second death
  Worthy it was to come unto this joy.

The other one, through grace, that from so deep
  A fountain wells that never hath the eye
  Of any creature reached its primal wave,

Set all his love below on righteousness;
  Wherefore from grace to grace did God unclose
  His eye to our redemption yet to be,

Whence he believed therein, and suffered not
  From that day forth the stench of paganism,
  And he reproved therefor the folk perverse.

Those Maidens three, whom at the right-hand wheel
  Thou didst behold, were unto him for baptism
  More than a thousand years before baptizing.

O thou predestination, how remote
  Thy root is from the aspect of all those
  Who the First Cause do not behold entire!

And you, O mortals! hold yourselves restrained
  In judging; for ourselves, who look on God,
  We do not know as yet all the elect;

And sweet to us is such a deprivation,
  Because our good in this good is made perfect,
  That whatsoe'er God wills, we also will."

After this manner by that shape divine,
  To make clear in me my short-sightedness,
  Was given to me a pleasant medicine;

And as good singer a good lutanist
  Accompanies with vibrations of the chords,
  Whereby more pleasantness the song acquires,

So, while it spake, do I remember me
  That I beheld both of those blessed lights,
  Even as the winking of the eyes concords,

Moving unto the words their little flames.

Canto XXI

Already on my Lady's face mine eyes
  Again were fastened, and with these my mind,
  And from all other purpose was withdrawn;

And she smiled not; but "If I were to smile,"
  She unto me began, "thou wouldst become
  Like Semele, when she was turned to ashes.

Because my beauty, that along the stairs
  Of the eternal palace more enkindles,
  As thou hast seen, the farther we ascend,

If it were tempered not, is so resplendent
  That all thy mortal power in its effulgence
  Would seem a leaflet that the thunder crushes.

We are uplifted to the seventh splendor,
  That underneath the burning Lion's breast
  Now radiates downward mingled with his power.

Fix in direction of thine eyes the mind,
  And make of them a mirror for the figure
  That in this mirror shall appear to thee."

He who could know what was the pasturage
  My sight had in that blessed countenance,
  When I transferred me to another care,

Would recognize how grateful was to me
  Obedience unto my celestial escort,
  By counterpoising one side with the other.

Within the crystal which, around the world
  Revolving, bears the name of its dear leader,
  Under whom every wickedness lay dead,

Colored like gold, on which the sunshine gleams,
  A stairway I beheld to such a height
  Uplifted, that mine eye pursued it not.

Likewise beheld I down the steps descending
  So many splendors, that I thought each light
  That in the heaven appears was there diffused.

And as accordant with their natural custom
  The rooks together at the break of day
  Bestir themselves to warm their feathers cold;

Then some of them fly off without return,
  Others come back to where they started from,
  And others, wheeling round, still keep at home;

Such fashion it appeared to me was there
  Within the sparkling that together came,
  As soon as on a certain step it struck,

And that which nearest unto us remained
  Became so clear, that in my thought I said,
  "Well I perceive the love thou showest me;

But she, from whom I wait the how and when
  Of speech and silence, standeth still; whence I
  Against desire do well if I ask not."

She thereupon, who saw my silentness
  In the sight of Him who seeth everything,
  Said unto me, "Let loose thy warm desire."

And I began: "No merit of my own
  Renders me worthy of response from thee;
  But for her sake who granteth me the asking,

Thou blessed life that dost remain concealed
  In thy beatitude, make known to me
  The cause which draweth thee so near my side;

And tell me why is silent in this wheel
  The dulcet symphony of Paradise,
  That through the rest below sounds so devoutly."

"Thou hast thy hearing mortal as thy sight,"
  It answer made to me; "they sing not here,
  For the same cause that Beatrice has not smiled.

Thus far adown the holy stairway's steps
  Have I descended but to give thee welcome
  With words, and with the light that mantles me;

Nor did more love cause me to be more ready,
  For love as much and more up there is burning,
  As doth the flaming manifest to thee.

But the high charity, that makes us servants
  Prompt to the counsel which controls the world,
  Allotteth here, even as thou dost observe."

"I see full well," said I, "O sacred lamp!
  How love unfettered in this court sufficeth
  To follow the eternal Providence;

But this is what seems hard for me to see,
  Wherefore predestinate wast thou alone
  Unto this office from among thy consorts."

No sooner had I come to the last word,
  Than of its middle made the light a centre,
  Whirling itself about like a swift millstone.

When answer made the love that was therein:
  "On me directed is a light divine,
  Piercing through this in which I am embosomed,

Of which the virtue with my sight conjoined
  Lifts me above myself so far, I see
  The supreme essence from which this is drawn.

Hence comes the joyfulness with which I flame,
  For to my sight, as far as it is clear,
  The clearness of the flame I equal make.

But that soul in the heaven which is most pure,
  That seraph which his eye on God most fixes,
  Could this demand of thine not satisfy;

Because so deeply sinks in the abyss
  Of the eternal statute what thou askest,
  From all created sight it is cut off.

And to the mortal world, when thou returnest,
  This carry back, that it may not presume
  Longer tow'rd such a goal to move its feet.

The mind, that shineth here, on earth doth smoke;
  From this observe how can it do below
  That which it cannot though the heaven assume it?"

Such limit did its words prescribe to me,
  The question I relinquished, and restricted
  Myself to ask it humbly who it was.

"Between two shores of Italy rise cliffs,
  And not far distant from thy native place,
  So high, the thunders far below them sound,

And form a ridge that Catria is called,
  'Neath which is consecrate a hermitage
  Wont to be dedicate to worship only."

Thus unto me the third speech recommenced,
  And then, continuing, it said: "Therein
  Unto God's service I became so steadfast,

That feeding only on the juice of olives
  Lightly I passed away the heats and frosts,
  Contented in my thoughts contemplative.

That cloister used to render to these heavens
  Abundantly, and now is empty grown,
  So that perforce it soon must be revealed.

I in that place was Peter Damiano;
  And Peter the Sinner was I in the house
  Of Our Lady on the Adriatic shore.

Little of mortal life remained to me,
  When I was called and dragged forth to the hat
  Which shifteth evermore from bad to worse.

Came Cephas, and the mighty Vessel came
  Of the Holy Spirit, meagre and barefooted,
  Taking the food of any hostelry.

Now some one to support them on each side
  The modern shepherds need, and some to lead them,
  So heavy are they, and to hold their trains.

They cover up their palfreys with their cloaks,
  So that two beasts go underneath one skin;
  O Patience, that dost tolerate so much!"

At this voice saw I many little flames
  From step to step descending and revolving,
  And every revolution made them fairer.

Round about this one came they and stood still,
  And a cry uttered of so loud a sound,
  It here could find no parallel, nor I

Distinguished it, the thunder so o'ercame me.

Canto XXII

Oppressed with stupor, I unto my guide
  Turned like a little child who always runs
  For refuge there where he confideth most;

And she, even as a mother who straightway
  Gives comfort to her pale and breathless boy
  With voice whose wont it is to reassure him,

Said to me: "Knowest thou not thou art in heaven,
  And knowest thou not that heaven is holy all
  And what is done here cometh from good zeal?

After what wise the singing would have changed thee
  And I by smiling, thou canst now imagine,
  Since that the cry has startled thee so much,

In which if thou hadst understood its prayers
  Already would be known to thee the vengeance
  Which thou shalt look upon before thou diest.

The sword above here smiteth not in haste
  Nor tardily, howe'er it seem to him
  Who fearing or desiring waits for it.

But turn thee round towards the others now,
  For very illustrious spirits shalt thou see,
  If thou thy sight directest as I say."

As it seemed good to her mine eyes I turned,
  And saw a hundred spherules that together
  With mutual rays each other more embellished.

I stood as one who in himself represses
  The point of his desire, and ventures not
  To question, he so feareth the too much.

And now the largest and most luculent
  Among those pearls came forward, that it might
  Make my desire concerning it content.

Within it then I heard: "If thou couldst see
  Even as myself the charity that burns
  Among us, thy conceits would be expressed;

But, that by waiting thou mayst not come late
  To the high end, I will make answer even
  Unto the thought of which thou art so chary.

That mountain on whose slope Cassino stands
  Was frequented of old upon its summit
  By a deluded folk and ill-disposed;

And I am he who first up thither bore
  The name of Him who brought upon the earth
  The truth that so much sublimateth us.

And such abundant grace upon me shone
  That all the neighboring towns I drew away
  From the impious worship that seduced the world.

These other fires, each one of them, were men
  Contemplative, enkindled by that heat
  Which maketh holy flowers and fruits spring up.

Here is Macarius, here is Romualdus,
  Here are my brethren, who within the cloisters
  Their footsteps stayed and kept a steadfast heart."

And I to him: "The affection which thou showest
  Speaking with me, and the good countenance
  Which I behold and note in all your ardours,

In me have so my confidence dilated
  As the sun doth the rose, when it becomes
  As far unfolded as it hath the power.

Therefore I pray, and thou assure me, father,
  If I may so much grace receive, that I
  May thee behold with countenance unveiled."

He thereupon: "Brother, thy high desire
  In the remotest sphere shall be fulfilled,
  Where are fulfilled all others and my own.

There perfect is, and ripened, and complete,
  Every desire; within that one alone
  Is every part where it has always been;

For it is not in space, nor turns on poles,
  And unto it our stairway reaches up,
  Whence thus from out thy sight it steals away.

Up to that height the Patriarch Jacob saw it
  Extending its supernal part, what time
  So thronged with angels it appeared to him.

But to ascend it now no one uplifts
  His feet from off the earth, and now my Rule
  Below remaineth for mere waste of paper.

The walls that used of old to be an Abbey
  Are changed to dens of robbers, and the cowls
  Are sacks filled full of miserable flour.

But heavy usury is not taken up
  So much against God's pleasure as that fruit
  Which maketh so insane the heart of monks;

For whatsoever hath the Church in keeping
  Is for the folk that ask it in God's name,
  Not for one's kindred or for something worse.

The flesh of mortals is so very soft,
  That good beginnings down below suffice not
  From springing of the oak to bearing acorns.

Peter began with neither gold nor silver,
  And I with orison and abstinence,
  And Francis with humility his convent.

And if thou lookest at each one's beginning,
  And then regardest whither he has run,
  Thou shalt behold the white changed into brown.

In verity the Jordan backward turned,
  And the sea's fleeing, when God willed were more
  A wonder to behold, than succor here."

Thus unto me he said; and then withdrew
  To his own band, and the band closed together;
  Then like a whirlwind all was upward rapt.

The gentle Lady urged me on behind them
  Up o'er that stairway by a single sign,
  So did her virtue overcome my nature;

Nor here below, where one goes up and down
  By natural law, was motion e'er so swift
  That it could be compared unto my wing.

Reader, as I may unto that devout
  Triumph return, on whose account I often
  For my transgressions weep and beat my breast,—

Thou hadst not thrust thy finger in the fire
  And drawn it out again, before I saw
  The sign that follows Taurus, and was in it.

O glorious stars, O light impregnated
  With mighty virtue, from which I acknowledge
  All of my genius, whatsoe'er it be,

With you was born, and hid himself with you,
  He who is father of all mortal life,
  When first I tasted of the Tuscan air;

And then when grace was freely given to me
  To enter the high wheel which turns you round,
  Your region was allotted unto me.

To you devoutly at this hour my soul
  Is sighing, that it virtue may acquire
  For the stern pass that draws it to itself.

"Thou art so near unto the last salvation,"
  Thus Beatrice began, "thou oughtest now
  To have thine eves unclouded and acute;

And therefore, ere thou enter farther in,
  Look down once more, and see how vast a world
  Thou hast already put beneath thy feet;

So that thy heart, as jocund as it may,
  Present itself to the triumphant throng
  That comes rejoicing through this rounded ether."

I with my sight returned through one and all
  The sevenfold spheres, and I beheld this globe
  Such that I smiled at its ignoble semblance;

And that opinion I approve as best
  Which doth account it least; and he who thinks
  Of something else may truly be called just.

I saw the daughter of Latona shining
  Without that shadow, which to me was cause
  That once I had believed her rare and dense.

The aspect of thy son, Hyperion,
  Here I sustained, and saw how move themselves
  Around and near him Maia and Dione.

Thence there appeared the temperateness of Jove
  'Twixt son and father, and to me was clear
  The change that of their whereabout they make;

And all the seven made manifest to me
  How great they are, and eke how swift they are,
  And how they are in distant habitations.

The threshing-floor that maketh us so proud,
  To me revolving with the eternal Twins,
  Was all apparent made from hill to harbour!

Then to the beauteous eyes mine eyes I turned.

Canto XXIII

Even as a bird, 'mid the beloved leaves,
  Quiet upon the nest of her sweet brood
  Throughout the night, that hideth all things from us,

Who, that she may behold their longed-for looks
  And find the food wherewith to nourish them,
  In which, to her, grave labours grateful are,

Anticipates the time on open spray
  And with an ardent longing waits the sun,
  Gazing intent as soon as breaks the dawn:

Even thus my Lady standing was, erect
  And vigilant, turned round towards the zone
  Underneath which the sun displays less haste;

So that beholding her distraught and wistful,
  Such I became as he is who desiring
  For something yearns, and hoping is appeased.

But brief the space from one When to the other;
  Of my awaiting, say I, and the seeing
  The welkin grow resplendent more and more.

And Beatrice exclaimed: "Behold the hosts
  Of Christ's triumphal march, and all the fruit
  Harvested by the rolling of these spheres!"

It seemed to me her face was all aflame;
  And eyes she had so full of ecstasy
  That I must needs pass on without describing.

As when in nights serene of the full moon
  Smiles Trivia among the nymphs eternal
  Who paint the firmament through all its gulfs,

Saw I, above the myriads of lamps,
  A Sun that one and all of them enkindled,
  E'en as our own doth the supernal sights,

And through the living light transparent shone
  The lucent substance so intensely clear
  Into my sight, that I sustained it not.

O Beatrice, thou gentle guide and dear!
  To me she said: "What overmasters thee
  A virtue is from which naught shields itself.

There are the wisdom and the omnipotence
  That oped the thoroughfares 'twixt heaven and earth,
  For which there erst had been so long a yearning."

As fire from out a cloud unlocks itself,
  Dilating so it finds not room therein,
  And down, against its nature, falls to earth,

So did my mind, among those aliments
  Becoming larger, issue from itself,
  And that which it became cannot remember.

"Open thine eyes, and look at what I am:
  Thou hast beheld such things, that strong enough
  Hast thou become to tolerate my smile."

I was as one who still retains the feeling
  Of a forgotten vision, and endeavours
  In vain to bring it back into his mind,

When I this invitation heard, deserving
  Of so much gratitude, it never fades
  Out of the book that chronicles the past.

If at this moment sounded all the tongues
  That Polyhymnia and her sisters made
  Most lubrical with their delicious milk,

To aid me, to a thousandth of the truth
  It would not reach, singing the holy smile
  And how the holy aspect it illumed.

And therefore, representing Paradise,
  The sacred poem must perforce leap over,
  Even as a man who finds his way cut off;

But whoso thinketh of the ponderous theme,
  And of the mortal shoulder laden with it,
  Should blame it not, if under this it tremble.

It is no passage for a little boat
  This which goes cleaving the audacious prow,
  Nor for a pilot who would spare himself.

"Why doth my face so much enamour thee,
  That to the garden fair thou turnest not,
  Which under the rays of Christ is blossoming?

There is the Rose in which the Word Divine
  Became incarnate; there the lilies are
  By whose perfume the good way was discovered."

Thus Beatrice; and I, who to her counsels
  Was wholly ready, once again betook me
  Unto the battle of the feeble brows.

As in the sunshine, that unsullied streams
  Through fractured cloud, ere now a meadow of flowers
  Mine eyes with shadow covered o'er have seen,

So troops of splendors manifold I saw
  Illumined from above with burning rays,
  Beholding not the source of the effulgence.

O power benignant that dost so imprint them!
  Thou didst exalt thyself to give more scope
  There to mine eyes, that were not strong enough.

The name of that fair flower I e'er invoke
  Morning and evening utterly enthralled
  My soul to gaze upon the greater fire.

And when in both mine eyes depicted were
  The glory and greatness of the living star
  Which there excelleth, as it here excelled,

Athwart the heavens a little torch descended
  Formed in a circle like a coronal,
  And cinctured it, and whirled itself about it.

Whatever melody most sweetly soundeth
  On earth, and to itself most draws the soul,
  Would seem a cloud that, rent asunder, thunders,

Compared unto the sounding of that lyre
  Wherewith was crowned the sapphire beautiful,
  Which gives the clearest heaven its sapphire hue.

"I am Angelic Love, that circle round
  The joy sublime which breathes from out the womb
  That was the hostelry of our Desire;

And I shall circle, Lady of Heaven, while
  Thou followest thy Son, and mak'st diviner
  The sphere supreme, because thou enterest there."

Thus did the circulated melody
  Seal itself up; and all the other lights
  Were making to resound the name of Mary.

The regal mantle of the volumes all
  Of that world, which most fervid is and living
  With breath of God and with his works and ways,

Extended over us its inner border,
  So very distant, that the semblance of it
  There where I was not yet appeared to me.

Therefore mine eyes did not possess the power
  Of following the incoronated flame,
  Which mounted upward near to its own seed.

And as a little child, that towards its mother
  Stretches its arms, when it the milk has taken,
  Through impulse kindled into outward flame,

Each of those gleams of whiteness upward reached
  So with its summit, that the deep affection
  They had for Mary was revealed to me.

Thereafter they remained there in my sight,
  'Regina coeli' singing with such sweetness,
  That ne'er from me has the delight departed.

O, what exuberance is garnered up
  Within those richest coffers, which had been
  Good husbandmen for sowing here below!

There they enjoy and live upon the treasure
  Which was acquired while weeping in the exile
  Of Babylon, wherein the gold was left.

There triumpheth, beneath the exalted Son
  Of God and Mary, in his victory,
  Both with the ancient council and the new,

He who doth keep the keys of such a glory.

Canto XXIV

"O company elect to the great supper
  Of the Lamb benedight, who feedeth you
  So that for ever full is your desire,

If by the grace of God this man foretaste
  Something of that which falleth from your table,
  Or ever death prescribe to him the time,

Direct your mind to his immense desire,
  And him somewhat bedew; ye drinking are
  For ever at the fount whence comes his thought."

Thus Beatrice; and those souls beatified
  Transformed themselves to spheres on steadfast poles,
  Flaming intensely in the guise of comets.

And as the wheels in works of horologes
  Revolve so that the first to the beholder
  Motionless seems, and the last one to fly,

So in like manner did those carols, dancing
  In different measure, of their affluence
  Give me the gauge, as they were swift or slow.

From that one which I noted of most beauty
  Beheld I issue forth a fire so happy
  That none it left there of a greater brightness;

And around Beatrice three several times
  It whirled itself with so divine a song,
  My fantasy repeats it not to me;

Therefore the pen skips, and I write it not,
  Since our imagination for such folds,
  Much more our speech, is of a tint too glaring.

"O holy sister mine, who us implorest
  With such devotion, by thine ardent love
  Thou dost unbind me from that beautiful sphere!"

Thereafter, having stopped, the blessed fire
  Unto my Lady did direct its breath,
  Which spake in fashion as I here have said.

And she: "O light eterne of the great man
  To whom our Lord delivered up the keys
  He carried down of this miraculous joy,

This one examine on points light and grave,
  As good beseemeth thee, about the Faith
  By means of which thou on the sea didst walk.

If he love well, and hope well, and believe,
  From thee 'tis hid not; for thou hast thy sight
  There where depicted everything is seen.

But since this kingdom has made citizens
  By means of the true Faith, to glorify it
  'Tis well he have the chance to speak thereof."

As baccalaureate arms himself, and speaks not
  Until the master doth propose the question,
  To argue it, and not to terminate it,

So did I arm myself with every reason,
  While she was speaking, that I might be ready
  For such a questioner and such profession.

"Say, thou good Christian; manifest thyself;
  What is the Faith?" Whereat I raised my brow
  Unto that light wherefrom was this breathed forth.

Then turned I round to Beatrice, and she
  Prompt signals made to me that I should pour
  The water forth from my internal fountain.

"May grace, that suffers me to make confession,"
  Began I, "to the great centurion,
  Cause my conceptions all to be explicit!"

And I continued: "As the truthful pen,
  Father, of thy dear brother wrote of it,
  Who put with thee Rome into the good way,

Faith is the substance of the things we hope for,
  And evidence of those that are not seen;
  And this appears to me its quiddity."

Then heard I: "Very rightly thou perceivest,
  If well thou understandest why he placed it
  With substances and then with evidences."

And I thereafterward: "The things profound,
  That here vouchsafe to me their apparition,
  Unto all eyes below are so concealed,

That they exist there only in belief,
  Upon the which is founded the high hope,
  And hence it takes the nature of a substance.

And it behoveth us from this belief
  To reason without having other sight,
  And hence it has the nature of evidence."

Then heard I: "If whatever is acquired
  Below by doctrine were thus understood,
  No sophist's subtlety would there find place."

Thus was breathed forth from that enkindled love;
  Then added: "Very well has been gone over
  Already of this coin the alloy and weight;

But tell me if thou hast it in thy purse?"
  And I: "Yes, both so shining and so round
  That in its stamp there is no peradventure."

Thereafter issued from the light profound
  That there resplendent was: "This precious jewel,
  Upon the which is every virtue founded,

Whence hadst thou it?" And I: "The large outpouring
  Of Holy Spirit, which has been diffused
  Upon the ancient parchments and the new,

A syllogism is, which proved it to me
  With such acuteness, that, compared therewith,
  All demonstration seems to me obtuse."

And then I heard: "The ancient and the new
  Postulates, that to thee are so conclusive,
  Why dost thou take them for the word divine?"

And I: "The proofs, which show the truth to me,
  Are the works subsequent, whereunto Nature
  Ne'er heated iron yet, nor anvil beat."

'Twas answered me: "Say, who assureth thee
  That those works ever were? the thing itself
  That must be proved, nought else to thee affirms it."

"Were the world to Christianity converted,"
I said, "withouten miracles, this one
Is such, the rest are not its hundredth part;

Because that poor and fasting thou didst enter
Into the field to sow there the good plant,
Which was a vine and has become a thorn!"

This being finished, the high, holy Court
Resounded through the spheres, "One God we praise!"
In melody that there above is chanted.

And then that Baron, who from branch to branch,
Examining, had thus conducted me,
Till the extremest leaves we were approaching,

Again began: "The Grace that dallying
Plays with thine intellect thy mouth has opened,
Up to this point, as it should opened be,

So that I do approve what forth emerged;
But now thou must express what thou believest,
And whence to thy belief it was presented."

"O holy father, spirit who beholdest
What thou believedst so that thou o'ercamest,
Towards the sepulchre, more youthful feet,"

Began I, "thou dost wish me in this place
The form to manifest of my prompt belief,
And likewise thou the cause thereof demandest.

And I respond: In one God I believe,
Sole and eterne, who moveth all the heavens
With love and with desire, himself unmoved;

And of such faith not only have I proofs
Physical and metaphysical, but gives them
Likewise the truth that from this place rains down

Through Moses, through the Prophets and the Psalms,
Through the Evangel, and through you, who wrote
After the fiery Spirit sanctified you;

In Persons three eterne believe, and these
  One essence I believe, so one and trine
  They bear conjunction both with 'sunt' and 'est.'

With the profound condition and divine
  Which now I touch upon, doth stamp my mind
  Ofttimes the doctrine evangelical.

This the beginning is, this is the spark
  Which afterwards dilates to vivid flame,
  And, like a star in heaven, is sparkling in me."

Even as a lord who hears what pleaseth him
  His servant straight embraces, gratulating
  For the good news as soon as he is silent;

So, giving me its benediction, singing,
  Three times encircled me, when I was silent,
  The apostolic light, at whose command

I spoken had, in speaking I so pleased him.

Canto XXV

If e'er it happen that the Poem Sacred,
  To which both heaven and earth have set their hand,
  So that it many a year hath made me lean,

O'ercome the cruelty that bars me out
  From the fair sheepfold, where a lamb I slumbered,
  An enemy to the wolves that war upon it,

With other voice forthwith, with other fleece
  Poet will I return, and at my font
  Baptismal will I take the laurel crown;

Because into the Faith that maketh known
  All souls to God there entered I, and then
  Peter for her sake thus my brow encircled.

Thereafterward towards us moved a light
  Out of that band whence issued the first-fruits
  Which of his vicars Christ behind him left,

And then my Lady, full of ecstasy,
  Said unto me: "Look, look! behold the Baron
  For whom below Galicia is frequented."

In the same way as, when a dove alights
  Near his companion, both of them pour forth,
  Circling about and murmuring, their affection,

So one beheld I by the other grand
  Prince glorified to be with welcome greeted,
  Lauding the food that there above is eaten.

But when their gratulations were complete,
  Silently 'coram me' each one stood still,
  So incandescent it o'ercame my sight.

Smiling thereafterwards, said Beatrice:
  "Illustrious life, by whom the benefactions
  Of our Basilica have been described,

Make Hope resound within this altitude;
  Thou knowest as oft thou dost personify it
  As Jesus to the three gave greater clearness."—

"Lift up thy head, and make thyself assured;
  For what comes hither from the mortal world
  Must needs be ripened in our radiance."

This comfort came to me from the second fire;
  Wherefore mine eyes I lifted to the hills,
  Which bent them down before with too great weight.

"Since, through his grace, our Emperor wills that thou
  Shouldst find thee face to face, before thy death,
  In the most secret chamber, with his Counts,

So that, the truth beholden of this court,
  Hope, which below there rightfully enamours,
  Thereby thou strengthen in thyself and others,

Say what it is, and how is flowering with it
  Thy mind, and say from whence it came to thee."
  Thus did the second light again continue.

And the Compassionate, who piloted
  The plumage of my wings in such high flight,
  Did in reply anticipate me thus:

"No child whatever the Church Militant
  Of greater hope possesses, as is written
  In that Sun which irradiates all our band;

Therefore it is conceded him from Egypt
  To come into Jerusalem to see,
  Or ever yet his warfare be completed.

The two remaining points, that not for knowledge
  Have been demanded, but that he report
  How much this virtue unto thee is pleasing,

To him I leave; for hard he will not find them,
  Nor of self-praise; and let him answer them;
  And may the grace of God in this assist him!"

As a disciple, who his teacher follows,
  Ready and willing, where he is expert,
  That his proficiency may be displayed,

"Hope," said I, "is the certain expectation
  Of future glory, which is the effect
  Of grace divine and merit precedent.

From many stars this light comes unto me;
  But he instilled it first into my heart
  Who was chief singer unto the chief captain.

'Sperent in te,' in the high Theody
  He sayeth, 'those who know thy name;' and who
  Knoweth it not, if he my faith possess?

Thou didst instil me, then, with his instilling
  In the Epistle, so that I am full,
  And upon others rain again your rain."

While I was speaking, in the living bosom
  Of that combustion quivered an effulgence,
  Sudden and frequent, in the guise of lightning;

Then breathed: "The love wherewith I am inflamed
  Towards the virtue still which followed me
  Unto the palm and issue of the field,

Wills that I breathe to thee that thou delight
  In her; and grateful to me is thy telling
  Whatever things Hope promises to thee."

And I: "The ancient Scriptures and the new
  The mark establish, and this shows it me,
  Of all the souls whom God hath made his friends.

Isaiah saith, that each one garmented
  In his own land shall be with twofold garments,
  And his own land is this delightful life.

Thy brother, too, far more explicitly,
  There where he treateth of the robes of white,
  This revelation manifests to us."

And first, and near the ending of these words,
  "Sperent in te" from over us was heard,
  To which responsive answered all the carols.

Thereafterward a light among them brightened,
  So that, if Cancer one such crystal had,
  Winter would have a month of one sole day.

And as uprises, goes, and enters the dance
  A winsome maiden, only to do honor
  To the new bride, and not from any failing,

Even thus did I behold the brightened splendor
  Approach the two, who in a wheel revolved
  As was beseeming to their ardent love.

Into the song and music there it entered;
  And fixed on them my Lady kept her look,
  Even as a bride silent and motionless.

"This is the one who lay upon the breast
  Of him our Pelican; and this is he
  To the great office from the cross elected."

My Lady thus; but therefore none the more
  Did move her sight from its attentive gaze
  Before or afterward these words of hers.

Even as a man who gazes, and endeavours
  To see the eclipsing of the sun a little,
  And who, by seeing, sightless doth become,

So I became before that latest fire,
  While it was said, "Why dost thou daze thyself
  To see a thing which here hath no existence?

Earth in the earth my body is, and shall be
  With all the others there, until our number
  With the eternal proposition tallies.

With the two garments in the blessed cloister
  Are the two lights alone that have ascended:
  And this shalt thou take back into your world."

And at this utterance the flaming circle
  Grew quiet, with the dulcet intermingling
  Of sound that by the trinal breath was made,

As to escape from danger or fatigue
  The oars that erst were in the water beaten
  Are all suspended at a whistle's sound.

Ah, how much in my mind was I disturbed,
  When I turned round to look on Beatrice,
  That her I could not see, although I was

Close at her side and in the Happy World!

Canto XXVI

While I was doubting for my vision quenched,
  Out of the flame refulgent that had quenched it
  Issued a breathing, that attentive made me,

Saying: "While thou recoverest the sense
  Of seeing which in me thou hast consumed,
  'Tis well that speaking thou shouldst compensate it.

Begin then, and declare to what thy soul
　Is aimed, and count it for a certainty,
　Sight is in thee bewildered and not dead;

Because the Lady, who through this divine
　Region conducteth thee, has in her look
　The power the hand of Ananias had."

I said: "As pleaseth her, or soon or late
　Let the cure come to eyes that portals were
　When she with fire I ever burn with entered.

The Good, that gives contentment to this Court,
　The Alpha and Omega is of all
　The writing that love reads me low or loud."

The selfsame voice, that taken had from me
　The terror of the sudden dazzlement,
　To speak still farther put it in my thought;

And said: "In verity with finer sieve
　Behoveth thee to sift; thee it behoveth
　To say who aimed thy bow at such a target."

And I: "By philosophic arguments,
　And by authority that hence descends,
　Such love must needs imprint itself in me;

For Good, so far as good, when comprehended
　Doth straight enkindle love, and so much greater
　As more of goodness in itself it holds;

Then to that Essence (whose is such advantage
　That every good which out of it is found
　Is nothing but a ray of its own light)

More than elsewhither must the mind be moved
　Of every one, in loving, who discerns
　The truth in which this evidence is founded.

Such truth he to my intellect reveals
　Who demonstrates to me the primal love
　Of all the sempiternal substances.

The voice reveals it of the truthful Author,
  Who says to Moses, speaking of Himself,
  'I will make all my goodness pass before thee.'

Thou too revealest it to me, beginning
  The loud Evangel, that proclaims the secret
  Of heaven to earth above all other edict."

And I heard say: "By human intellect
  And by authority concordant with it,
  Of all thy loves reserve for God the highest.

But say again if other cords thou feelest,
  Draw thee towards Him, that thou mayst proclaim
  With how many teeth this love is biting thee."

The holy purpose of the Eagle of Christ
  Not latent was, nay, rather I perceived
  Whither he fain would my profession lead.

Therefore I recommenced: "All of those bites
  Which have the power to turn the heart to God
  Unto my charity have been concurrent.

The being of the world, and my own being,
  The death which He endured that I may live,
  And that which all the faithful hope, as I do,

With the forementioned vivid consciousness
  Have drawn me from the sea of love perverse,
  And of the right have placed me on the shore.

The leaves, wherewith embowered is all the garden
  Of the Eternal Gardener, do I love
  As much as he has granted them of good."

As soon as I had ceased, a song most sweet
  Throughout the heaven resounded, and my Lady
  Said with the others, "Holy, holy, holy!"

And as at some keen light one wakes from sleep
  By reason of the visual spirit that runs
  Unto the splendor passed from coat to coat,

And he who wakes abhorreth what he sees,
  So all unconscious is his sudden waking,
  Until the judgment cometh to his aid,

So from before mine eyes did Beatrice
  Chase every mote with radiance of her own,
  That cast its light a thousand miles and more.

Whence better after than before I saw,
  And in a kind of wonderment I asked
  About a fourth light that I saw with us.

And said my Lady: "There within those rays
  Gazes upon its Maker the first soul
  That ever the first virtue did create."

Even as the bough that downward bends its top
  At transit of the wind, and then is lifted
  By its own virtue, which inclines it upward,

Likewise did I, the while that she was speaking,
  Being amazed, and then I was made bold
  By a desire to speak wherewith I burned.

And I began: "O apple, that mature
  Alone hast been produced, O ancient father,
  To whom each wife is daughter and daughter-in-law,

Devoutly as I can I supplicate thee
  That thou wouldst speak to me; thou seest my wish;
  And I, to hear thee quickly, speak it not."

Sometimes an animal, when covered, struggles
  So that his impulse needs must be apparent,
  By reason of the wrappage following it;

And in like manner the primeval soul
  Made clear to me athwart its covering
  How jubilant it was to give me pleasure.

Then breathed: "Without thy uttering it to me,
  Thine inclination better I discern
  Than thou whatever thing is surest to thee;

For I behold it in the truthful mirror,
  That of Himself all things parhelion makes,
  And none makes Him parhelion of itself.

Thou fain wouldst hear how long ago God placed me
  Within the lofty garden, where this Lady
  Unto so long a stairway thee disposed.

And how long to mine eyes it was a pleasure,
  And of the great disdain the proper cause,
  And the language that I used and that I made.

Now, son of mine, the tasting of the tree
  Not in itself was cause of so great exile,
  But solely the o'erstepping of the bounds.

There, whence thy Lady moved Virgilius,
  Four thousand and three hundred and two circuits
  Made by the sun, this Council I desired;

And him I saw return to all the lights
  Of his highway nine hundred times and thirty,
  Whilst I upon the earth was tarrying.

The language that I spake was quite extinct
  Before that in the work interminable
  The people under Nimrod were employed;

For nevermore result of reasoning
  (Because of human pleasure that doth change,
  Obedient to the heavens) was durable.

A natural action is it that man speaks;
  But whether thus or thus, doth nature leave
  To your own art, as seemeth best to you.

Ere I descended to the infernal anguish,
  'El' was on earth the name of the Chief Good,
  From whom comes all the joy that wraps me round

'Eli' he then was called, and that is proper,
  Because the use of men is like a leaf
  On bough, which goeth and another cometh.

Upon the mount that highest o'er the wave
  Rises was I, in life or pure or sinful,
  From the first hour to that which is the second,

As the sun changes quadrant, to the sixth."

Canto XXVII

"Glory be to the Father, to the Son,
  And Holy Ghost!" all Paradise began,
  So that the melody inebriate made me.

What I beheld seemed unto me a smile
  Of the universe; for my inebriation
  Found entrance through the hearing and the sight.

O joy! O gladness inexpressible!
  O perfect life of love and peacefulness!
  O riches without hankering secure!

Before mine eyes were standing the four torches
  Enkindled, and the one that first had come
  Began to make itself more luminous;

And even such in semblance it became
  As Jupiter would become, if he and Mars
  Were birds, and they should interchange their feathers.

That Providence, which here distributeth
  Season and service, in the blessed choir
  Had silence upon every side imposed.

When I heard say: "If I my color change,
  Marvel not at it; for while I am speaking
  Thou shalt behold all these their color change.

He who usurps upon the earth my place,
  My place, my place, which vacant has become
  Before the presence of the Son of God,

Has of my cemetery made a sewer
  Of blood and stench, whereby the Perverse One,
  Who fell from here, below there is appeased!"

With the same color which, through sun adverse,
  Painteth the clouds at evening or at morn,
  Beheld I then the whole of heaven suffused.

And as a modest woman, who abides
  Sure of herself, and at another's failing,
  From listening only, timorous becomes,

Even thus did Beatrice change countenance;
  And I believe in heaven was such eclipse,
  When suffered the supreme Omnipotence;

Thereafterward proceeded forth his words
  With voice so much transmuted from itself,
  The very countenance was not more changed.

"The spouse of Christ has never nurtured been
  On blood of mine, of Linus and of Cletus,
  To be made use of in acquest of gold;

But in acquest of this delightful life
  Sixtus and Pius, Urban and Calixtus,
  After much lamentation, shed their blood.

Our purpose was not, that on the right hand
  Of our successors should in part be seated
  The Christian folk, in part upon the other;

Nor that the keys which were to me confided
  Should e'er become the escutcheon on a banner,
  That should wage war on those who are baptized;

Nor I be made the figure of a seal
  To privileges venal and mendacious,
  Whereat I often redden and flash with fire.

In garb of shepherds the rapacious wolves
  Are seen from here above o'er all the pastures!
  O wrath of God, why dost thou slumber still?

To drink our blood the Caorsines and Gascons
  Are making ready. O thou good beginning,
  Unto how vile an end must thou needs fall!

But the high Providence, that with Scipio
  At Rome the glory of the world defended,
  Will speedily bring aid, as I conceive;

And thou, my son, who by thy mortal weight
  Shalt down return again, open thy mouth;
  What I conceal not, do not thou conceal."

As with its frozen vapours downward falls
  In flakes our atmosphere, what time the horn
  Of the celestial Goat doth touch the sun,

Upward in such array saw I the ether
  Become, and flaked with the triumphant vapours,
  Which there together with us had remained.

My sight was following up their semblances,
  And followed till the medium, by excess,
  The passing farther onward took from it;

Whereat the Lady, who beheld me freed
  From gazing upward, said to me: "Cast down
  Thy sight, and see how far thou art turned round."

Since the first time that I had downward looked,
  I saw that I had moved through the whole arc
  Which the first climate makes from midst to end;

So that I saw the mad track of Ulysses
  Past Gades, and this side, well nigh the shore
  Whereon became Europa a sweet burden.

And of this threshing-floor the site to me
  Were more unveiled, but the sun was proceeding
  Under my feet, a sign and more removed.

My mind enamoured, which is dallying
  At all times with my Lady, to bring back
  To her mine eyes was more than ever ardent.

And if or Art or Nature has made bait
  To catch the eyes and so possess the mind,
  In human flesh or in its portraiture,

All joined together would appear as nought
  To the divine delight which shone upon me
  When to her smiling face I turned me round.

The virtue that her look endowed me with
  From the fair nest of Leda tore me forth,
  And up into the swiftest heaven impelled me.

Its parts exceeding full of life and lofty
  Are all so uniform, I cannot say
  Which Beatrice selected for my place.

But she, who was aware of my desire,
  Began, the while she smiled so joyously
  That God seemed in her countenance to rejoice:

"The nature of that motion, which keeps quiet
  The centre and all the rest about it moves,
  From hence begins as from its starting point.

And in this heaven there is no other Where
  Than in the Mind Divine, wherein is kindled
  The love that turns it, and the power it rains.

Within a circle light and love embrace it,
  Even as this doth the others, and that precinct
  He who encircles it alone controls.

Its motion is not by another meted,
  But all the others measured are by this,
  As ten is by the half and by the fifth.

And in what manner time in such a pot
  May have its roots, and in the rest its leaves,
  Now unto thee can manifest be made.

O Covetousness, that mortals dost ingulf
  Beneath thee so, that no one hath the power
  Of drawing back his eyes from out thy waves!

Full fairly blossoms in mankind the will;
  But the uninterrupted rain converts
  Into abortive wildings the true plums.

Fidelity and innocence are found
  Only in children; afterwards they both
  Take flight or e'er the cheeks with down are covered.

One, while he prattles still, observes the fasts,
  Who, when his tongue is loosed, forthwith devours
  Whatever food under whatever moon;

Another, while he prattles, loves and listens
  Unto his mother, who when speech is perfect
  Forthwith desires to see her in her grave.

Even thus is swarthy made the skin so white
  In its first aspect of the daughter fair
  Of him who brings the morn, and leaves the night.

Thou, that it may not be a marvel to thee,
  Think that on earth there is no one who governs;
  Whence goes astray the human family.

Ere January be unwintered wholly
  By the centesimal on earth neglected,
  Shall these supernal circles roar so loud

The tempest that has been so long awaited
  Shall whirl the poops about where are the prows;
  So that the fleet shall run its course direct,

And the true fruit shall follow on the flower."

Canto XXVIII

After the truth against the present life
  Of miserable mortals was unfolded
  By her who doth imparadise my mind,

As in a looking-glass a taper's flame
  He sees who from behind is lighted by it,
  Before he has it in his sight or thought,

And turns him round to see if so the glass
  Tell him the truth, and sees that it accords
  Therewith as doth a music with its metre,

In similar wise my memory recollecteth
  That I did, looking into those fair eyes,
  Of which Love made the springes to ensnare me.

And as I turned me round, and mine were touched
  By that which is apparent in that volume,
  Whenever on its gyre we gaze intent,

A point beheld I, that was raying out
  Light so acute, the sight which it enkindles
  Must close perforce before such great acuteness.

And whatsoever star seems smallest here
  Would seem to be a moon, if placed beside it.
  As one star with another star is placed.

Perhaps at such a distance as appears
  A halo cincturing the light that paints it,
  When densest is the vapour that sustains it,

Thus distant round the point a circle of fire
  So swiftly whirled, that it would have surpassed
  Whatever motion soonest girds the world;

And this was by another circumcinct,
  That by a third, the third then by a fourth,
  By a fifth the fourth, and then by a sixth the fifth;

The seventh followed thereupon in width
  So ample now, that Juno's messenger
  Entire would be too narrow to contain it.

Even so the eighth and ninth; and every one
  More slowly moved, according as it was
  In number distant farther from the first.

And that one had its flame most crystalline
  From which less distant was the stainless spark,
  I think because more with its truth imbued.

My Lady, who in my anxiety
  Beheld me much perplexed, said: "From that point
  Dependent is the heaven and nature all.

Behold that circle most conjoined to it,
  And know thou, that its motion is so swift
  Through burning love whereby it is spurred on."

And I to her: "If the world were arranged
  In the order which I see in yonder wheels,
  What's set before me would have satisfied me;

But in the world of sense we can perceive
  That evermore the circles are diviner
  As they are from the centre more remote

Wherefore if my desire is to be ended
  In this miraculous and angelic temple,
  That has for confines only love and light,

To hear behoves me still how the example
  And the exemplar go not in one fashion,
  Since for myself in vain I contemplate it."

"If thine own fingers unto such a knot
  Be insufficient, it is no great wonder,
  So hard hath it become for want of trying."

My Lady thus; then said she: "Do thou take
  What I shall tell thee, if thou wouldst be sated,
  And exercise on that thy subtlety.

The circles corporal are wide and narrow
  According to the more or less of virtue
  Which is distributed through all their parts.

The greater goodness works the greater weal,
  The greater weal the greater body holds,
  If perfect equally are all its parts.

Therefore this one which sweeps along with it
  The universe sublime, doth correspond
  Unto the circle which most loves and knows.

On which account, if thou unto the virtue
  Apply thy measure, not to the appearance
  Of substances that unto thee seem round,

Thou wilt behold a marvellous agreement,
  Of more to greater, and of less to smaller,
  In every heaven, with its Intelligence."

Even as remaineth splendid and serene
  The hemisphere of air, when Boreas
  Is blowing from that cheek where he is mildest,

Because is purified and resolved the rack
  That erst disturbed it, till the welkin laughs
  With all the beauties of its pageantry;

Thus did I likewise, after that my Lady
  Had me provided with her clear response,
  And like a star in heaven the truth was seen.

And soon as to a stop her words had come,
  Not otherwise does iron scintillate
  When molten, than those circles scintillated.

Their coruscation all the sparks repeated,
  And they so many were, their number makes
  More millions than the doubling of the chess.

I heard them sing hosanna choir by choir
  To the fixed point which holds them at the 'Ubi,'
  And ever will, where they have ever been.

And she, who saw the dubious meditations
  Within my mind, "The primal circles," said,
  "Have shown thee Seraphim and Cherubim.

Thus rapidly they follow their own bonds,
  To be as like the point as most they can,
  And can as far as they are high in vision.

Those other Loves, that round about them go,
  Thrones of the countenance divine are called,
  Because they terminate the primal Triad.

And thou shouldst know that they all have delight
  As much as their own vision penetrates
  The Truth, in which all intellect finds rest.

From this it may be seen how blessedness
    Is founded in the faculty which sees,
    And not in that which loves, and follows next;

And of this seeing merit is the measure,
    Which is brought forth by grace, and by good will;
    Thus on from grade to grade doth it proceed.

The second Triad, which is germinating
    In such wise in this sempiternal spring,
    That no nocturnal Aries despoils,

Perpetually hosanna warbles forth
    With threefold melody, that sounds in three
    Orders of joy, with which it is intrined.

The three Divine are in this hierarchy,
    First the Dominions, and the Virtues next;
    And the third order is that of the Powers.

Then in the dances twain penultimate
    The Principalities and Archangels wheel;
    The last is wholly of angelic sports.

These orders upward all of them are gazing,
    And downward so prevail, that unto God
    They all attracted are and all attract.

And Dionysius with so great desire
    To contemplate these Orders set himself,
    He named them and distinguished them as I do.

But Gregory afterwards dissented from him;
    Wherefore, as soon as he unclosed his eyes
    Within this heaven, he at himself did smile.

And if so much of secret truth a mortal
    Proffered on earth, I would not have thee marvel,
    For he who saw it here revealed it to him,

With much more of the truth about these circles."

Canto XXIX

At what time both the children of Latona,
  Surmounted by the Ram and by the Scales,
  Together make a zone of the horizon,

As long as from the time the zenith holds them
  In equipoise, till from that girdle both
  Changing their hemisphere disturb the balance,

So long, her face depicted with a smile,
  Did Beatrice keep silence while she gazed
  Fixedly at the point which had o'ercome me.

Then she began: "I say, and I ask not
  What thou dost wish to hear, for I have seen it
  Where centres every When and every 'Ubi.'

Not to acquire some good unto himself,
  Which is impossible, but that his splendor
  In its resplendency may say, 'Subsisto,'

In his eternity outside of time,
  Outside all other limits, as it pleased him,
  Into new Loves the Eternal Love unfolded.

Nor as if torpid did he lie before;
  For neither after nor before proceeded
  The going forth of God upon these waters.

Matter and Form unmingled and conjoined
  Came into being that had no defect,
  E'en as three arrows from a three-stringed bow.

And as in glass, in amber, or in crystal
  A sunbeam flashes so, that from its coming
  To its full being is no interval,

So from its Lord did the triform effect
  Ray forth into its being all together,
  Without discrimination of beginning.

Order was con-created and constructed
  In substances, and summit of the world
  Were those wherein the pure act was produced.

Pure potentiality held the lowest part;
  Midway bound potentiality with act
  Such bond that it shall never be unbound.

Jerome has written unto you of angels
  Created a long lapse of centuries
  Or ever yet the other world was made;

But written is this truth in many places
  By writers of the Holy Ghost, and thou
  Shalt see it, if thou lookest well thereat.

And even reason seeth it somewhat,
  For it would not concede that for so long
  Could be the motors without their perfection.

Now dost thou know both where and when these Loves
  Created were, and how; so that extinct
  In thy desire already are three fires.

Nor could one reach, in counting, unto twenty
  So swiftly, as a portion of these angels
  Disturbed the subject of your elements.

The rest remained, and they began this art
  Which thou discernest, with so great delight
  That never from their circling do they cease.

The occasion of the fall was the accursed
  Presumption of that One, whom thou hast seen
  By all the burden of the world constrained.

Those whom thou here beholdest modest were
  To recognize themselves as of that goodness
  Which made them apt for so much understanding;

On which account their vision was exalted
  By the enlightening grace and their own merit,
  So that they have a full and steadfast will.

I would not have thee doubt, but certain be,
'Tis meritorious to receive this grace,
According as the affection opens to it.

Now round about in this consistory
Much mayst thou contemplate, if these my words
Be gathered up, without all further aid.

But since upon the earth, throughout your schools,
They teach that such is the angelic nature
That it doth hear, and recollect, and will,

More will I say, that thou mayst see unmixed
The truth that is confounded there below,
Equivocating in such like prelections.

These substances, since in God's countenance
They jocund were, turned not away their sight
From that wherefrom not anything is hidden;

Hence they have not their vision intercepted
By object new, and hence they do not need
To recollect, through interrupted thought.

So that below, not sleeping, people dream,
Believing they speak truth, and not believing;
And in the last is greater sin and shame.

Below you do not journey by one path
Philosophising; so transporteth you
Love of appearance and the thought thereof.

And even this above here is endured
With less disdain, than when is set aside
The Holy Writ, or when it is distorted.

They think not there how much of blood it costs
To sow it in the world, and how he pleases
Who in humility keeps close to it.

Each striveth for appearance, and doth make
His own inventions; and these treated are
By preachers, and the Evangel holds its peace.

One sayeth that the moon did backward turn,
  In the Passion of Christ, and interpose herself
  So that the sunlight reached not down below;

And lies; for of its own accord the light
  Hid itself; whence to Spaniards and to Indians,
  As to the Jews, did such eclipse respond.

Florence has not so many Lapi and Bindi
  As fables such as these, that every year
  Are shouted from the pulpit back and forth,

In such wise that the lambs, who do not know,
  Come back from pasture fed upon the wind,
  And not to see the harm doth not excuse them.

Christ did not to his first disciples say,
  'Go forth, and to the world preach idle tales,'
  But unto them a true foundation gave;

And this so loudly sounded from their lips,
  That, in the warfare to enkindle Faith,
  They made of the Evangel shields and lances.

Now men go forth with jests and drolleries
  To preach, and if but well the people laugh,
  The hood puffs out, and nothing more is asked.

But in the cowl there nestles such a bird,
  That, if the common people were to see it,
  They would perceive what pardons they confide in,

For which so great on earth has grown the folly,
  That, without proof of any testimony,
  To each indulgence they would flock together.

By this Saint Anthony his pig doth fatten,
  And many others, who are worse than pigs,
  Paying in money without mark of coinage.

But since we have digressed abundantly,
  Turn back thine eyes forthwith to the right path,
  So that the way be shortened with the time.

This nature doth so multiply itself
  In numbers, that there never yet was speech
  Nor mortal fancy that can go so far.

And if thou notest that which is revealed
  By Daniel, thou wilt see that in his thousands
  Number determinate is kept concealed.

The primal light, that all irradiates it,
  By modes as many is received therein,
  As are the splendors wherewith it is mated.

Hence, inasmuch as on the act conceptive
  The affection followeth, of love the sweetness
  Therein diversely fervid is or tepid.

The height behold now and the amplitude
  Of the eternal power, since it hath made
  Itself so many mirrors, where 'tis broken,

One in itself remaining as before."

Canto XXX

Perchance six thousand miles remote from us
  Is glowing the sixth hour, and now this world
  Inclines its shadow almost to a level,

When the mid-heaven begins to make itself
  So deep to us, that here and there a star
  Ceases to shine so far down as this depth,

And as advances bright exceedingly
  The handmaid of the sun, the heaven is closed
  Light after light to the most beautiful;

Not otherwise the Triumph, which for ever
  Plays round about the point that vanquished me,
  Seeming enclosed by what itself encloses,

Little by little from my vision faded;
  Whereat to turn mine eyes on Beatrice
  My seeing nothing and my love constrained me.

If what has hitherto been said of her
  Were all concluded in a single praise,
  Scant would it be to serve the present turn.

Not only does the beauty I beheld
  Transcend ourselves, but truly I believe
  Its Maker only may enjoy it all.

Vanquished do I confess me by this passage
  More than by problem of his theme was ever
  O'ercome the comic or the tragic poet;

For as the sun the sight that trembles most,
  Even so the memory of that sweet smile
  My mind depriveth of its very self.

From the first day that I beheld her face
  In this life, to the moment of this look,
  The sequence of my song has ne'er been severed;

But now perforce this sequence must desist
  From following her beauty with my verse,
  As every artist at his uttermost.

Such as I leave her to a greater fame
  Than any of my trumpet, which is bringing
  Its arduous matter to a final close,

With voice and gesture of a perfect leader
  She recommenced: "We from the greatest body
  Have issued to the heaven that is pure light;

Light intellectual replete with love,
  Love of true good replete with ecstasy,
  Ecstasy that transcendeth every sweetness.

Here shalt thou see the one host and the other
  Of Paradise, and one in the same aspects
  Which at the final judgment thou shalt see."

Even as a sudden lightning that disperses
  The visual spirits, so that it deprives
  The eye of impress from the strongest objects,

Thus round about me flashed a living light,
  And left me swathed around with such a veil
  Of its effulgence, that I nothing saw.

"Ever the Love which quieteth this heaven
  Welcomes into itself with such salute,
  To make the candle ready for its flame."

No sooner had within me these brief words
  An entrance found, than I perceived myself
  To be uplifted over my own power,

And I with vision new rekindled me,
  Such that no light whatever is so pure
  But that mine eyes were fortified against it.

And light I saw in fashion of a river
  Fulvid with its effulgence, 'twixt two banks
  Depicted with an admirable Spring.

Out of this river issued living sparks,
  And on all sides sank down into the flowers,
  Like unto rubies that are set in gold;

And then, as if inebriate with the odours,
  They plunged again into the wondrous torrent,
  And as one entered issued forth another.

"The high desire, that now inflames and moves thee
  To have intelligence of what thou seest,
  Pleaseth me all the more, the more it swells.

But of this water it behoves thee drink
  Before so great a thirst in thee be slaked."
  Thus said to me the sunshine of mine eyes;

And added: "The river and the topazes
  Going in and out, and the laughing of the herbage,
  Are of their truth foreshadowing prefaces;

Not that these things are difficult in themselves,
  But the deficiency is on thy side,
  For yet thou hast not vision so exalted."

There is no babe that leaps so suddenly
  With face towards the milk, if he awake
  Much later than his usual custom is,

As I did, that I might make better mirrors
  Still of mine eyes, down stooping to the wave
  Which flows that we therein be better made.

And even as the penthouse of mine eyelids
  Drank of it, it forthwith appeared to me
  Out of its length to be transformed to round.

Then as a folk who have been under masks
  Seem other than before, if they divest
  The semblance not their own they disappeared in,

Thus into greater pomp were changed for me
  The flowerets and the sparks, so that I saw
  Both of the Courts of Heaven made manifest.

O splendor of God! by means of which I saw
  The lofty triumph of the realm veracious,
  Give me the power to say how it I saw!

There is a light above, which visible
  Makes the Creator unto every creature,
  Who only in beholding Him has peace,

And it expands itself in circular form
  To such extent, that its circumference
  Would be too large a girdle for the sun.

The semblance of it is all made of rays
  Reflected from the top of Primal Motion,
  Which takes therefrom vitality and power.

And as a hill in water at its base
  Mirrors itself, as if to see its beauty
  When affluent most in verdure and in flowers,

So, ranged aloft all round about the light,
  Mirrored I saw in more ranks than a thousand
  All who above there have from us returned.

And if the lowest row collect within it
  So great a light, how vast the amplitude
  Is of this Rose in its extremest leaves!

My vision in the vastness and the height
  Lost not itself, but comprehended all
  The quantity and quality of that gladness.

There near and far nor add nor take away;
  For there where God immediately doth govern,
  The natural law in naught is relevant.

Into the yellow of the Rose Eternal
  That spreads, and multiplies, and breathes an odour
  Of praise unto the ever-vernal Sun,

As one who silent is and fain would speak,
  Me Beatrice drew on, and said: "Behold
  Of the white stoles how vast the convent is!

Behold how vast the circuit of our city!
  Behold our seats so filled to overflowing,
  That here henceforward are few people wanting!

On that great throne whereon thine eyes are fixed
  For the crown's sake already placed upon it,
  Before thou suppest at this wedding feast

Shall sit the soul (that is to be Augustus
  On earth) of noble Henry, who shall come
  To redress Italy ere she be ready.

Blind covetousness, that casts its spell upon you,
  Has made you like unto the little child,
  Who dies of hunger and drives off the nurse.

And in the sacred forum then shall be
  A Prefect such, that openly or covert
  On the same road he will not walk with him.

But long of God he will not be endured
  In holy office; he shall be thrust down
  Where Simon Magus is for his deserts,

And make him of Alagna lower go!"

Canto XXXI

In fashion then as of a snow-white rose
  Displayed itself to me the saintly host,
  Whom Christ in his own blood had made his bride,

But the other host, that flying sees and sings
  The glory of Him who doth enamour it,
  And the goodness that created it so noble,

Even as a swarm of bees, that sinks in flowers
  One moment, and the next returns again
  To where its labour is to sweetness turned,

Sank into the great flower, that is adorned
  With leaves so many, and thence reascended
  To where its love abideth evermore.

Their faces had they all of living flame,
  And wings of gold, and all the rest so white
  No snow unto that limit doth attain.

From bench to bench, into the flower descending,
  They carried something of the peace and ardour
  Which by the fanning of their flanks they won.

Nor did the interposing 'twixt the flower
  And what was o'er it of such plenitude
  Of flying shapes impede the sight and splendor;

Because the light divine so penetrates
  The universe, according to its merit,
  That naught can be an obstacle against it.

This realm secure and full of gladsomeness,
  Crowded with ancient people and with modern,
  Unto one mark had all its look and love.

O Trinal Light, that in a single star
  Sparkling upon their sight so satisfies them,
  Look down upon our tempest here below!

If the barbarians, coming from some region
  That every day by Helice is covered,
  Revolving with her son whom she delights in,

Beholding Rome and all her noble works,
  Were wonder-struck, what time the Lateran
  Above all mortal things was eminent,—

I who to the divine had from the human,
  From time unto eternity, had come,
  From Florence to a people just and sane,

With what amazement must I have been filled!
  Truly between this and the joy, it was
  My pleasure not to hear, and to be mute.

And as a pilgrim who delighteth him
  In gazing round the temple of his vow,
  And hopes some day to retell how it was,

So through the living light my way pursuing
  Directed I mine eyes o'er all the ranks,
  Now up, now down, and now all round about.

Faces I saw of charity persuasive,
  Embellished by His light and their own smile,
  And attitudes adorned with every grace.

The general form of Paradise already
  My glance had comprehended as a whole,
  In no part hitherto remaining fixed,

And round I turned me with rekindled wish
  My Lady to interrogate of things
  Concerning which my mind was in suspense.

One thing I meant, another answered me;
  I thought I should see Beatrice, and saw
  An Old Man habited like the glorious people.

O'erflowing was he in his eyes and cheeks
  With joy benign, in attitude of pity
  As to a tender father is becoming.

And "She, where is she?" instantly I said;
  Whence he: "To put an end to thy desire,
  Me Beatrice hath sent from mine own place.

And if thou lookest up to the third round
  Of the first rank, again shalt thou behold her
  Upon the throne her merits have assigned her."

Without reply I lifted up mine eyes,
  And saw her, as she made herself a crown
  Reflecting from herself the eternal rays.

Not from that region which the highest thunders
  Is any mortal eye so far removed,
  In whatsoever sea it deepest sinks,

As there from Beatrice my sight; but this
  Was nothing unto me; because her image
  Descended not to me by medium blurred.

"O Lady, thou in whom my hope is strong,
  And who for my salvation didst endure
  In Hell to leave the imprint of thy feet,

Of whatsoever things I have beheld,
  As coming from thy power and from thy goodness
  I recognize the virtue and the grace.

Thou from a slave hast brought me unto freedom,
  By all those ways, by all the expedients,
  Whereby thou hadst the power of doing it.

Preserve towards me thy magnificence,
  So that this soul of mine, which thou hast healed,
  Pleasing to thee be loosened from the body."

Thus I implored; and she, so far away,
  Smiled, as it seemed, and looked once more at me;
  Then unto the eternal fountain turned.

And said the Old Man holy: "That thou mayst
  Accomplish perfectly thy journeying,
  Whereunto prayer and holy love have sent me,

Fly with thine eyes all round about this garden;
 For seeing it will discipline thy sight
 Farther to mount along the ray divine.

And she, the Queen of Heaven, for whom I burn
 Wholly with love, will grant us every grace,
 Because that I her faithful Bernard am."

As he who peradventure from Croatia
 Cometh to gaze at our Veronica,
 Who through its ancient fame is never sated,

But says in thought, the while it is displayed,
 "My Lord, Christ Jesus, God of very God,
 Now was your semblance made like unto this?"

Even such was I while gazing at the living
 Charity of the man, who in this world
 By contemplation tasted of that peace.

"Thou son of grace, this jocund life," began he,
 "Will not be known to thee by keeping ever
 Thine eyes below here on the lowest place;

But mark the circles to the most remote,
 Until thou shalt behold enthroned the Queen
 To whom this realm is subject and devoted."

I lifted up mine eyes, and as at morn
 The oriental part of the horizon
 Surpasses that wherein the sun goes down,

Thus, as if going with mine eyes from vale
 To mount, I saw a part in the remoteness
 Surpass in splendor all the other front.

And even as there where we await the pole
 That Phaeton drove badly, blazes more
 The light, and is on either side diminished,

So likewise that pacific oriflamme
 Gleamed brightest in the centre, and each side
 In equal measure did the flame abate.

And at that centre, with their wings expanded,
  More than a thousand jubilant Angels saw I,
  Each differing in effulgence and in kind.

I saw there at their sports and at their songs
  A beauty smiling, which the gladness was
  Within the eyes of all the other saints;

And if I had in speaking as much wealth
  As in imagining, I should not dare
  To attempt the smallest part of its delight.

Bernard, as soon as he beheld mine eyes
  Fixed and intent upon its fervid fervour,
  His own with such affection turned to her

That it made mine more ardent to behold.

Canto XXXII

Absorbed in his delight, that contemplator
  Assumed the willing office of a teacher,
  And gave beginning to these holy words:

"The wound that Mary closed up and anointed,
  She at her feet who is so beautiful,
  She is the one who opened it and pierced it.

Within that order which the third seats make
  Is seated Rachel, lower than the other,
  With Beatrice, in manner as thou seest.

Sarah, Rebecca, Judith, and her who was
  Ancestress of the Singer, who for dole
  Of the misdeed said, 'Miserere mei,'

Canst thou behold from seat to seat descending
  Down in gradation, as with each one's name
  I through the Rose go down from leaf to leaf.

And downward from the seventh row, even as
  Above the same, succeed the Hebrew women,
  Dividing all the tresses of the flower;

Because, according to the view which Faith
In Christ had taken, these are the partition
By which the sacred stairways are divided.

Upon this side, where perfect is the flower
With each one of its petals, seated are
Those who believed in Christ who was to come.

Upon the other side, where intersected
With vacant spaces are the semicircles,
Are those who looked to Christ already come.

And as, upon this side, the glorious seat
Of the Lady of Heaven, and the other seats
Below it, such a great division make,

So opposite doth that of the great John,
Who, ever holy, desert and martyrdom
Endured, and afterwards two years in Hell.

And under him thus to divide were chosen
Francis, and Benedict, and Augustine,
And down to us the rest from round to round.

Behold now the high providence divine;
For one and other aspect of the Faith
In equal measure shall this garden fill.

And know that downward from that rank which cleaves
Midway the sequence of the two divisions,
Not by their proper merit are they seated;

But by another's under fixed conditions;
For these are spirits one and all assoiled
Before they any true election had.

Well canst thou recognize it in their faces,
And also in their voices puerile,
If thou regard them well and hearken to them.

Now doubtest thou, and doubting thou art silent;
But I will loosen for thee the strong bond
In which thy subtile fancies hold thee fast.

Within the amplitude of this domain
  No casual point can possibly find place,
  No more than sadness can, or thirst, or hunger;

For by eternal law has been established
  Whatever thou beholdest, so that closely
  The ring is fitted to the finger here.

And therefore are these people, festinate
  Unto true life, not 'sine causa' here
  More and less excellent among themselves.

The King, by means of whom this realm reposes
  In so great love and in so great delight
  That no will ventureth to ask for more,

In his own joyous aspect every mind
  Creating, at his pleasure dowers with grace
  Diversely; and let here the effect suffice.

And this is clearly and expressly noted
  For you in Holy Scripture, in those twins
  Who in their mother had their anger roused.

According to the color of the hair,
  Therefore, with such a grace the light supreme
  Consenteth that they worthily be crowned.

Without, then, any merit of their deeds,
  Stationed are they in different gradations,
  Differing only in their first acuteness.

'Tis true that in the early centuries,
  With innocence, to work out their salvation
  Sufficient was the faith of parents only.

After the earlier ages were completed,
  Behoved it that the males by circumcision
  Unto their innocent wings should virtue add;

But after that the time of grace had come
  Without the baptism absolute of Christ,
  Such innocence below there was retained.

Look now into the face that unto Christ
  Hath most resemblance; for its brightness only
  Is able to prepare thee to see Christ."

On her did I behold so great a gladness
  Rain down, borne onward in the holy minds
  Created through that altitude to fly,

That whatsoever I had seen before
  Did not suspend me in such admiration,
  Nor show me such similitude of God.

And the same Love that first descended there,
  "Ave Maria, gratia plena," singing,
  In front of her his wings expanded wide.

Unto the canticle divine responded
  From every part the court beatified,
  So that each sight became serener for it.

"O holy father, who for me endurest
  To be below here, leaving the sweet place
  In which thou sittest by eternal lot,

Who is the Angel that with so much joy
  Into the eyes is looking of our Queen,
  Enamoured so that he seems made of fire?"

Thus I again recourse had to the teaching
  Of that one who delighted him in Mary
  As doth the star of morning in the sun.

And he to me: "Such gallantry and grace
  As there can be in Angel and in soul,
  All is in him; and thus we fain would have it;

Because he is the one who bore the palm
  Down unto Mary, when the Son of God
  To take our burden on himself decreed.

But now come onward with thine eyes, as I
  Speaking shall go, and note the great patricians
  Of this most just and merciful of empires.

Those two that sit above there most enrapture
  As being very near unto Augusta,
  Are as it were the two roots of this Rose.

He who upon the left is near her placed
  The father is, by whose audacious taste
  The human species so much bitter tastes.

Upon the right thou seest that ancient father
  Of Holy Church, into whose keeping Christ
  The keys committed of this lovely flower.

And he who all the evil days beheld,
  Before his death, of her the beauteous bride
  Who with the spear and with the nails was won,

Beside him sits, and by the other rests
  That leader under whom on manna lived
  The people ingrate, fickle, and stiff-necked.

Opposite Peter seest thou Anna seated,
  So well content to look upon her daughter,
  Her eyes she moves not while she sings Hosanna.

And opposite the eldest household father
  Lucia sits, she who thy Lady moved
  When to rush downward thou didst bend thy brows.

But since the moments of thy vision fly,
  Here will we make full stop, as a good tailor
  Who makes the gown according to his cloth,

And unto the first Love will turn our eyes,
  That looking upon Him thou penetrate
  As far as possible through his effulgence.

Truly, lest peradventure thou recede,
  Moving thy wings believing to advance,
  By prayer behoves it that grace be obtained;

Grace from that one who has the power to aid thee;
  And thou shalt follow me with thy affection
  That from my words thy heart turn not aside."

And he began this holy orison.

Canto XXXIII

"Thou Virgin Mother, daughter of thy Son,
  Humble and high beyond all other creature,
  The limit fixed of the eternal counsel,

Thou art the one who such nobility
  To human nature gave, that its Creator
  Did not disdain to make himself its creature.

Within thy womb rekindled was the love,
  By heat of which in the eternal peace
  After such wise this flower has germinated.

Here unto us thou art a noonday torch
  Of charity, and below there among mortals
  Thou art the living fountain-head of hope.

Lady, thou art so great, and so prevailing,
  That he who wishes grace, nor runs to thee,
  His aspirations without wings would fly.

Not only thy benignity gives succor
  To him who asketh it, but oftentimes
  Forerunneth of its own accord the asking.

In thee compassion is, in thee is pity,
  In thee magnificence; in thee unites
  Whate'er of goodness is in any creature.

Now doth this man, who from the lowest depth
  Of the universe as far as here has seen
  One after one the spiritual lives,

Supplicate thee through grace for so much power
  That with his eyes he may uplift himself
  Higher towards the uttermost salvation.

And I, who never burned for my own seeing
  More than I do for his, all of my prayers
  Proffer to thee, and pray they come not short,

That thou wouldst scatter from him every cloud
Of his mortality so with thy prayers,
That the Chief Pleasure be to him displayed.

Still farther do I pray thee, Queen, who canst
Whate'er thou wilt, that sound thou mayst preserve
After so great a vision his affections.

Let thy protection conquer human movements;
See Beatrice and all the blessed ones
My prayers to second clasp their hands to thee!"

The eyes beloved and revered of God,
Fastened upon the speaker, showed to us
How grateful unto her are prayers devout;

Then unto the Eternal Light they turned,
On which it is not credible could be
By any creature bent an eye so clear.

And I, who to the end of all desires
Was now approaching, even as I ought
The ardour of desire within me ended.

Bernard was beckoning unto me, and smiling,
That I should upward look; but I already
Was of my own accord such as he wished;

Because my sight, becoming purified,
Was entering more and more into the ray
Of the High Light which of itself is true.

From that time forward what I saw was greater
Than our discourse, that to such vision yields,
And yields the memory unto such excess.

Even as he is who seeth in a dream,
And after dreaming the imprinted passion
Remains, and to his mind the rest returns not,

Even such am I, for almost utterly
Ceases my vision, and distilleth yet
Within my heart the sweetness born of it;

Even thus the snow is in the sun unsealed,
Even thus upon the wind in the light leaves
Were the soothsayings of the Sibyl lost.

O Light Supreme, that dost so far uplift thee
From the conceits of mortals, to my mind
Of what thou didst appear re-lend a little,

And make my tongue of so great puissance,
That but a single sparkle of thy glory
It may bequeath unto the future people;

For by returning to my memory somewhat,
And by a little sounding in these verses,
More of thy victory shall be conceived!

I think the keenness of the living ray
Which I endured would have bewildered me,
If but mine eyes had been averted from it;

And I remember that I was more bold
On this account to bear, so that I joined
My aspect with the Glory Infinite.

O grace abundant, by which I presumed
To fix my sight upon the Light Eternal,
So that the seeing I consumed therein!

I saw that in its depth far down is lying
Bound up with love together in one volume,
What through the universe in leaves is scattered;

Substance, and accident, and their operations,
All interfused together in such wise
That what I speak of is one simple light.

The universal fashion of this knot
Methinks I saw, since more abundantly
In saying this I feel that I rejoice.

One moment is more lethargy to me,
Than five and twenty centuries to the emprise
That startled Neptune with the shade of Argo!

My mind in this wise wholly in suspense,
Steadfast, immovable, attentive gazed,
And evermore with gazing grew enkindled.

In presence of that light one such becomes,
That to withdraw therefrom for other prospect
It is impossible he e'er consent;

Because the good, which object is of will,
Is gathered all in this, and out of it
That is defective which is perfect there.

Shorter henceforward will my language fall
Of what I yet remember, than an infant's
Who still his tongue doth moisten at the breast.

Not because more than one unmingled semblance
Was in the living light on which I looked,
For it is always what it was before;

But through the sight, that fortified itself
In me by looking, one appearance only
To me was ever changing as I changed.

Within the deep and luminous subsistence
Of the High Light appeared to me three circles,
Of threefold color and of one dimension,

And by the second seemed the first reflected
As Iris is by Iris, and the third
Seemed fire that equally from both is breathed.

O how all speech is feeble and falls short
Of my conceit, and this to what I saw
Is such, 'tis not enough to call it little!

O Light Eterne, sole in thyself that dwellest,
Sole knowest thyself, and, known unto thyself
And knowing, lovest and smilest on thyself!

That circulation, which being thus conceived
Appeared in thee as a reflected light,
When somewhat contemplated by mine eyes,

Within itself, of its own very color
  Seemed to me painted with our effigy,
  Wherefore my sight was all absorbed therein.

As the geometrician, who endeavours
  To square the circle, and discovers not,
  By taking thought, the principle he wants,

Even such was I at that new apparition;
  I wished to see how the image to the circle
  Conformed itself, and how it there finds place;

But my own wings were not enough for this,
  Had it not been that then my mind there smote
  A flash of lightning, wherein came its wish.

Here vigour failed the lofty fantasy:
  But now was turning my desire and will,
  Even as a wheel that equally is moved,

The Love which moves the sun and the other stars.

THE END

www.ingramcontent.com/pod-product-compliance
Lightning Source LLC
Chambersburg PA
CBHW022130170626
46808CB00002B/931